FESTIVAL

a novel by

Richard G. Edwards

Front Cover
Cover photo by the author is of the Harlan County, Kentucky Court House. The picture was taken from Central Street, directly in front of Creech Cafe (aka Creech Drug Store).

Acknowledgements

I want to sincerely thank Dr. Bill Green, Mr. Jack Sterling, Dr. Gus Peters, and my wife Carolyn for providing many excellent suggestions, comments, and corrections for this novel. Dr. Carl Peters, pastor of my church, Anchor Baptist, in Lexington, Kentucky provided several stories for Mayor Fred Knapp. Fred thanks you Carl!

Mrs. Kelly Elliott did the expert layout of the book, as well as those for my previous 8 novels. What a blessing she is, and greatly appreciated!

Dedication

Tom Schrodt was a dear friend. Tragically, he passed away on December 16, 2019 after being struck head-on by a driver who crossed the median and hit his car on Friday, December 13th. Dr. James Thomas Schrodt was a professor emeritus in Chemical Engineering at the University of Kentucky, an avid outdoorsman, and world-class Rainbow Trout fisherman. He authored the authoritative guide titled ***Fly Fishing in Kentucky***. Tom had lunch each week with a group of friends called ROMEOs, **R**etired **O**ld **M**en **E**ating **O**ut. His wit and knowledge were always shared, and so deeply appreciated. We all enjoyed greatly our association with him, his lovely wife Rita, and super family. We sure miss Tom.

Preface

This is my ninth novel. The first five (***Anchor Cross Series***), the sixth (***Nuclear Attack***), the seventh (***The Adventures of Preacher Puss***), the eighth (***Black Mountain Deception***), and this current one (***Festival***) each have many of the same mountain characters, and are all set in Harlan County, Kentucky. I've tried my best to include a lot of mountain stories and humor reflecting my Kentucky mountain heritage, of which I'm very proud. I've received lots of feedback from those reading my books, and I truly value it. If you have not read my prior novels see their titles listed below. They are all available from Amazon.com and Barnesandnoble.com, or directly from me by just sending a request to my email, as follows:

RICHARDGLENNEDWARDS@GMAIL.COM

I would also greatly value any comments you might care to share with me.

A list of my previous books:

1. *Anchor Cross Second Edition*
2. *The Pelle Anchor Cross*
3. *The Helena Anchor Cross*
4. *The Anchor Cross Twins*
5. *The Constantine Anchor Cross*
6. *Nuclear Attack*
7. *The Adventures of Preacher Puss*
8. *Black Mountain Deception*

Author's Note

All my previous novels are based in my beloved hometown of Harlan, Kentucky. The first five books constitute what I call "The Anchor Cross Series". It revolves about six mysterious and powerful golden anchor crosses that were produced by the Roman Emperor Constantine the Great around 325 AD from a bar of gold given to him by the then Pope, Sylvester I. The gold bar was one of many that had originally been blessed by our Lord Jesus Christ and then given to St. Peter to start His church. Each book in the Anchor Cross Series describes the story of one, or in the case of the fourth book (The Anchor Cross Twins) two, of these mysterious golden Anchor Crosses. The last four of my novels have continued with many of the same characters. Festival will be the last with them. Although all are fictional, I have come to closely associate with each and hope that you, my readers, have enjoyed them as well.

Please be aware that in *Festival* I identify sections with the day, time, and location the events take place. In some sections I designate the time or date as being "earlier". This is always relative to the prior section, e.g. chapter 2 begins "5 months earlier", meaning 5 months earlier than the event at the end of chapter 1.

Prologue

About 18 years ago a ten year old boy named Kyle
Potter was out exploring in the woods of Harlan County, Kentucky when he stumbled across the remains of a
horse-drawn wagon that Reverand Karl Seibert and his
wife Mary were riding in the 1790's on their way to the
new settlement called Mount Pleasant, later renamed Harlan, Kentucky. Unfortunately, Indians attacked and killed
them. Stirring through the rotted remains of the wooden
wagon parts Kyle came across a beautiful golden artifact. It was cast in the shape of an anchor cross and was
about 4 inches in width along the horizontal cross arm,
6 inches along the vertical cross member, and about 1/2
inch thick.....all solid gold! Kyle showed it to his mother
Carolyn, and she contacted their pastor, the Reverend
Raymond Bell for advice. Pastor Bell phoned his friend
Dr. Randy Peters, Director of the Center for Appalachian
Research at the University of Kentucky in Lexington.
After examining the artifact, Dr. Peters' research found
that the anchor cross was likely one of six that dated back
to the early fourth century and had been made by the

Roman Emperor Constantine the Great. The horizontal arm of the anchor cross had the Latin words Pax Tecum, meaning "peace be with you", cast in it. Kyle's anchor cross over the next few months exhibited some very mysterious and unexplained properties. On one occasion Kyle's drunken father in a fit of rage grabbed a baseball bat and swung it intending to hit Kyle's mom Carolyn in the head, Kyle, with the anchor cross in his pocket, reached up with his arm to deflect the bat. Just before striking Kyle's arm the bat suddenly bounced back and struck Kyle's drunken father in the forehead knocking him unconscious. Kyle suddenly felt something hot in his pocket. He reached in and pulled out the golden anchor cross. And then there was the incident where Kyle was wearing his anchor cross while visiting his mom at a bank where she worked. An attempted robbery took place and the bad guys were stopped when unexplained bolts of lightning struck them as they attempted to lock Carolyn and Kyle, along with several others, into the vault before leaving with 3.5 million dollars in drug money that had been deposited in the bank vault. Again, Kyle felt the anchor cross grow very warm when this happened. It was determined by the court that Kyle was responsible for saving the 3.5 million dollars and they awarded him 1.5 million of the drug money to be placed in a trust fund,

1 million to be used to construct a building on the court house property that would be called the Seibert Memorial and would tell the anchor cross story, and 1 million was awarded to Dr. Peters' Center for Appalachian Research to conduct further study related to the mysterious properties and history of the anchor cross.

For the next 12 years little additional information on the anchor cross was discovered. And then a second one was found in Prato, Italy. The world wide press coverage associated with this second anchor cross discovery resulted in a third being found soon after on the island of Mahe in the Seychelles, two more surfaced in Spain, and the sixth and final anchor cross was discovered off the Italian island of Ponza. Additional research conducted by Dr. Peters revealed that the origin of the gold bar Constantine used for molding the six artifacts could be traced all the way back to Saint Peter. Our Lord Jesus Christ had blessed many such golden bars and then given them to Saint Peter to start His church. The gold was passed down from one Pope to the next until in 325 AD Constantine shared with Pope Sylvester I his vision of a golden anchor cross that would be a Christian symbol. Up until this time the anchor had been used as a religious symbol going back to well before the time of Christ. Before and after Jesus died on the cross that form of punishment was reserved for only the worst and most despised criminals, and therefore the sign of the cross during those times was thought of very negatively. In his vision Constantine wanted to change this, and with the anchor cross he combined the two religious symbols. Perhaps Constantine was guided by two scriptures. Hebrews 6:19 says "We have this hope as an anchor of the soul, sure and steadfast", and First Corinthians 1:18 says, "For the message of the cross is foolishness to those who are perishing, but to us who are being saved it is the power of God". The Pope agreed with Constantine's vision and gave the Emperor one of Saint Peter's golden bars to use, and that one bar was sufficient to mold six of the beautiful anchor crosses. Constantine kept only one, gave the remaining five to Pope Sylvester I, and the six anchor crosses got passed down through the ages and eventually were found in various areas around the globe.

Because Dr. Randy Peters and his Center for Appalachian Research had become the recognized authority on the anchor crosses, all of the owners of the artifacts allowed him to borrow them for further study. Thus all six were now in his possession and kept in the Center at the University of Kentucky in Lexington. Dr. Peters had interviewed extensively each owner and had thus come to understand that all the artifacts apparently had very mysterious powers that could somehow protect those possessing them from harm, but this was only true if the protection accomplished a peaceful and just resolution. They provided no protection for evil purposes. And when this protection was invoked apparently energy was somehow passed through the artifacts that caused them to generate heat and feel very warm. About 5 years ago, after the discovery of the two anchor crosses in Madrid, Spain, it was suggested to the Governor of Kentucky that there should be established an annual festival in Harlan, Kentucky to allow the public to view the anchor crosses and to publicize their history and importance. It was suggested that the festival be called the ACFes, short for Anchor Cross Festival, and be held the first weekend of October each year. It would be highlighted by parades, speeches, and music by various celebrities and musicians, and a public display of the anchor crosses in the Seibert Memorial building on the grounds of the Harlan County Court House. The governor approved and provided funds to help support the festival and all of the anchor cross owners okayed their being transported to Harlan for festival viewing with the only stipulation being that a high degree of security would always be provided. Thus for the past four years a very successful ACFes has been held. This year will be ACFesV

Harlan, Kentucky is a small town nestled in the mountains of Eastern Kentucky. In 1940 its population exceeded 5,000, and that of Harlan County over 80,000. Coal mining provided the economy. In more recent years the decline in demand for coal and the introduction of automated mining techniques have drastically reduced the county's population and economy. The town of Harlan has a population today of only about 1,500. The county is now down to around 30,000. The annual Anchor Cross Festival provides a brief, welcome relief from an otherwise drab existence for the county's population. For the first weekend in October each year thousands of people come to celebrate ACFes. The economy booms. And Harlan Mayor Fred Knapp is one happy camper. Fred is not only the mayor, but he also owns a restaurant, Creech Cafe, directly across Central Street from the Harlan County Court House. Creech Cafe is a very popular hangout for young and old alike. After school each day lots of kids come to Fred's restaurant to eat snacks and socialize with friends. During school hours many of the old timers come to Creech's to drink coffee, spin tales, and get caught up on the latest town gossip. The restaurant has two unusual features. One is a large, green parrot named Polly that usually perches on a rod mounted above and to the side of the front door. Polly has quite a vocabulary, and is a very smart bird. She recognizes customers and frequently will greet them when they enter or exit. She also loves to mooch, and will fly through the cafe and land on a customer's shoulder, arm, or table and beg for food. All the locals know and accept her. The other unusual feature at Creech's is the walls. They are plastered with photographs and clippings from newspapers and magazines that Fred has thought worthy to grace his walls. Fred loves to explain any of these to those curious enough to ask. Fred loves people, and he enjoys greatly telling stories and jokes. He can spend hours talking about any of the pictures or articles on his store walls. Fred is loved by the people of Harlan, and has not been opposed in any mayoral election for many years.

A recent new employee hired by Fred is a fellow named Bennie Sekao. For most of his life Bennie was Harlan's town drunk. About a year ago Bennie was given a job working as a clerk for what turned out to be a very subversive company located on Black Mountain in Harlan County. Although he was hired because the company thought him just a stupid drunk, and they were only looking for someone to answer the phone and file papers, Bennie took the job very seriously and gave up drinking and turned out to be a superb employee. When the company's true evil purpose was discovered and it was eliminated, Bennie lost his job. Mayor Fred knew this story and decided to hire Bennie as Assistant Manager at Creech Drug. So far he has proven to be a great employee.

A daily customer at Creech's is the Harlan County Sheriff, Mr. J. Bert Sterling. Bert is extremely well liked and respected. He's 65 years old....ten years younger than Mayor Knapp. Chief Deputy Kyle Potter frequently accompanies Bert. Kyle, now 28 years old, found the original anchor cross when he was 10 years old. He decided he wanted to serve the people of Harlan County and attended and graduated from the Law Enforcement Program at Eastern Kentucky State University in Richmond. Sheriff Sterling was delighted to appoint him his chief deputy. Kyle is highly qualified and also greatly respected. Kyle's mother, Carolyn, and Bert are very close friends and have dated for years.

The Sheriff's Office, directly across the street from Creech Cafe, is located in the Harlan County Court House. Because of its limited budget, due largely to the continually decreasing tax base, the sheriff's office is small and only open sixteen hours per day (two shifts) Monday through Saturday, and only 8 hours on Sunday. Calls to the sheriff's office when it's closed are diverted to the Kentucky State Police Post 10 located in Harlan. In addition to the sheriff and chief deputy there are only two other deputies on duty for the first shift. Deputy Rosie Cain is stationed behind the counter and serves anyone walking into the office. The other deputy on the first shift is Simpson Brown. Simpson is usually on patrol in a cruiser. On the second shift are deputies Mousy Giles and Bill Black. Mousy usually works the office and Bill patrols in a cruiser. The sheriff's office also has a satellite operation located in Cumberland, Kentucky, about 25 miles Northeast of Harlan on Route 119. This office also has a total of 5 deputies.

One other very noteworthy occupant in the sheriff's office has four legs, is gray, and weighs about 17 pounds. Her name is Preacher Puss, and not only is she the resident mascot, but she is also an honorary deputy sheriff. She is truly a remarkable and unusual cat. She was brought to the sheriff's office by a fireman about 18 years ago. She had gotten herself trapped in a rural church that caught fire. When the fireman arrived they heard her screaming in a back room and rescued her. Deputy Rosie Cain had always been an animal lover, and when the fireman brought the cat into the sheriff's office Rosie immediately adopted her, naming her Preacher Puss after hearing the fireman's story of how she was found screaming in a burning church. She was built a shelf with a soft bed above Chief Deputy Potter's desk, near the office front door. The cat spends most of her time snoozing on the shelf while listening and occasionally opening an eye to keep informed as to what's going on. Since she was a kitten when found, Preacher Puss is now approaching 19 years old. But she is still in great shape, thanks largely to the excellent care provided her by Rosie. The cat had been involved in a very terrible incident when as a young kitten she was roaming in the woods and came across two other cats. While the cats were sniffing and hissing each other as cats do upon a first encounter, from a nearby dilapidated house a man came out the back door carrying what Preacher Puss later learned was called a pistol. When he came near the three cats he raised the gun and started shooting. With bullets landing all around her Preach-er Puss ran as fast as she could and managed to escape unharmed. But she still remembers the two other cats that were killed by the mean man with the pistol. That sad memory has remained with Preacher Puss all her life, and anytime anyone around her draws a pistol she immediate-ly reacts by doing whatever she can to make the person drop the gun. Usually this involves her jumping with claws extended from all four paws onto the arm or hand of the person and digging in with the claws until the gun is dropped. Over the years she has done this on many,

many occasions, and consequently has stopped many bad guys from using their guns unlawfully. She is recognized by all the citizens of Harlan County and law enforcement throughout the state for her unique ability to subdue crooks. Because of this, she has been officially recognized as an honorary deputy sheriff. She has saved countless lives since taking up residence in the sheriff's office. She is indeed a very, very special cat.

Another interesting Harlan County establishment is located about 10 miles South of Harlan on highway 119, near the town of Wallins. Maggard's Grocery is a small building. The primary room is stocked with groceries, and is maintained by Fatso Chapel. But Maggard's Grocery has very few customers because it is really just a front for many illegal operations carried out by the owner, Trigger Green. Trigger has an office in a back room. The door to the office has an electronic lock that is controlled by a button under the cash register. If anyone wanting to see Trigger was approved by Fatso he would press the button to allow the visitor to go back into Trigger's office. Trigger was involved in all kinds of illegal activities. Drugs, stolen credit cards, moonshine, stolen cars, stolen merchandise, and about anything else to make a buck. He had become the owner when the original owner, Pretty Boy Maggard, was discovered to have stashed 3.5 million dollars of drug money into a Harlan Bank. Pretty Boy escaped to Knoxville, Tennessee and has been operating from a junk yard there to cover his illegal activities. Trigger, while involved in all sorts of shady activity, usually manages to keep everything under cover and seldom runs into trouble with the law. In fact, Trigger really has a soft heart, and will not do anything to knowingly cause harm to anyone. He and Sheriff Sterling actually are friends, although Bert is well aware that Trigger is involved in unlawful activity....he just can't catch him at it. Fatso Chapel, Trigger's only employee, spends 90% of his time on a chair behind the check-out counter reading books and magazines or watching television on a small set above the cash register. Most people try to avoid Fatso because he loves to tell corny jokes. Anyone coming into Maggard's usually has to listen to one or more of Fatso's corny jokes, and those that know him try to avoid being exposed to these. Like Trigger, Fatso is basically a good hearted person, but a little slow. He's been an employee at Maggard's for many years and is very loyal to Trigger. He is aware of all the legal and illegal activity occurring there.

About midway between Harlan and Cumberland on highway 119 there is a 50 acre farm, the entrance to which is located several miles off the highway. The farm is owned by the Slusher Brothers, nicknamed Gunsmoke and Booger. They are very wealthy. Gunsmoke had won 100 million dollars in the national lottery and had elected to keep this a secret, and could since it was before it became mandatory for winners names to be made public. He and his brother Booger bought the 50 acre farm and live a very secluded and private life. They have three employees. Charlie and George work shifts on the main gate, only allowing anyone to enter that has proper business or has been requested by one of the brothers. Charlie works 6 am to 3 pm, George works 3 pm to midnight. After midnight the gate is locked and can not be entered unless for an emergency. The third employee is Ray. He provides security by guarding the perimeter of the property, runs errands as directed by the brothers, does some of the cooking, and does chores as needed. Gunsmoke and Booger are great lovers of cats. They have lost count as to how many they have. They frequently visit the animal shelter, and most often come home with one or more new cats. Preacher Puss had actually been one of these, although she had originally been named Smoky by the brothers. She wondered out the main gate one day when Charlie wasn't looking while the gate had been opened for a delivery, and had gotten lost wondering in the woods. After a couple of days she wondered upon the mean man with the pistol, and from there she wondered to the church building where she entered when the cleaning crew left the back door ajar.

In addition to the 3 employees and humpteen cats, the Slusher Brothers now have 10 very unusual additional folks living and working at their farm. These are ex-soldiers from North Korea that had at various times been sent to Harlan County at the direction of Supreme Leader Kim Jong-un. Kim had devised schemes to attempt to steal the anchor crosses during the ACFes and when these failed he wanted revenge and had sent other soldiers with orders to kill the North Koreans now working at the Slusher Farm after Sheriff Sterling had determined they were simply following Kim's orders and were good, hard-working people and had gotten them political asylum. These attempts also failed, and then Kim tried two other attacks. One involved launching a cruise-type missile with a nuclear weapon. The other was to launch from Harlan County a suborbital rocket carrying a nuclear warhead that, when exploded 100 miles above the earth, would cause a disastrous and deadly electromagnetic pulse. Both plots failed. Kim Jong-un was very mad and frustrated.

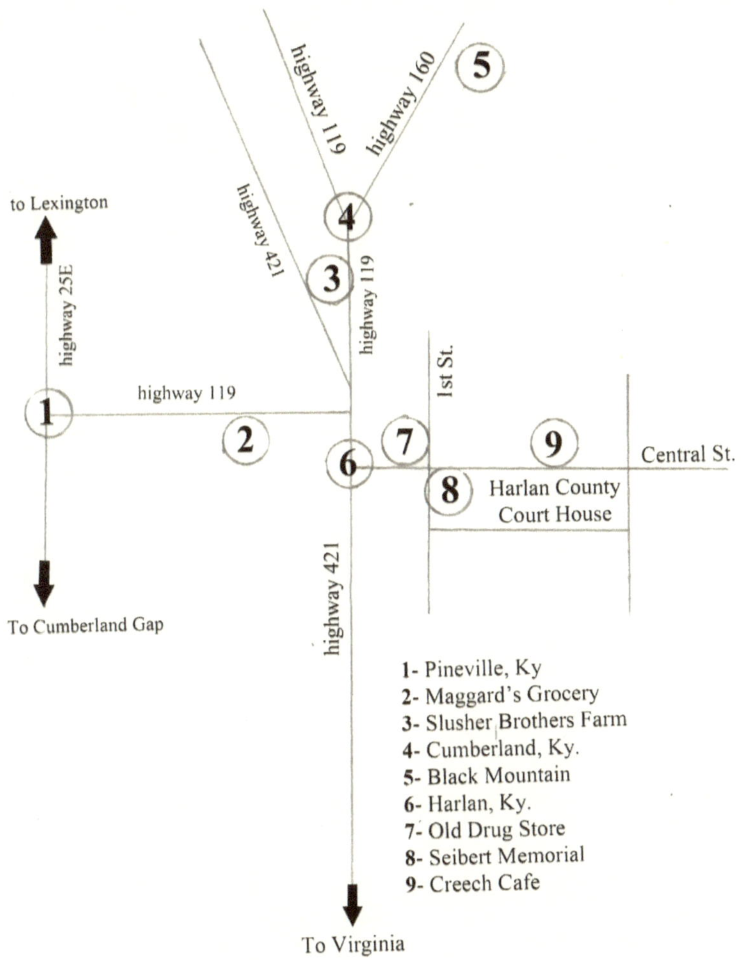

1- Pineville, Ky
2- Maggard's Grocery
3- Slusher Brothers Farm
4- Cumberland, Ky.
5- Black Mountain
6- Harlan, Ky.
7- Old Drug Store
8- Seibert Memorial
9- Creech Cafe

Map showing points of interest (not to scale)

Chapter 1

Present Time
Monday, June 15th, 9 am
Harlan, Kentucky

I t's the law! It's the law," squawked Polly as Sheriff J. Bert Sterling and his chief deputy Kyle Potter walked through the door at Creech Cafe in their crisp uniforms.

Bert reached up, stroked the parrot, and said, "Rest easy Polly, we're not going to arrest you!"

"Thank you! Thank you!" replied the bird.

Kyle saluted Polly as the two lawmen walked on into the cafe and headed toward a table.

"Hey Bert, hey Kyle," came a voice from behind the counter. "You guys grab your table and I'll be there with coffee."

"Thanks Bennie," replied the sheriff. "And I'll take a couple of doughnuts. How about you Kyle?"

Kyle rubbed his tummy and replied, "Why not? I need the energy!"

As they took their seats the cafe owner and mayor of Harlan, Fred Knapp, appeared from behind the office door in the back and hurried over to join the two. Fred said, "Morning gents. You two look all official and ready to start the week.....course you can only do that after you've had your morning coffee here at Creech's."

Bennie Sekao appeared at their table carrying a carafe of coffee on a tray with three cups and two dishes containing two doughnuts each. He placed the cups on the table, poured the coffee, and sat a dish of doughnuts in front of Bert and Kyle.

Kyle said, "Thanks Bennie, that'll get us off to a great start."

Bennie replied, "You're very welcome. Fred, you want doughnuts?"

"No, I've already had a couple Bennie."

"Okay boss, you guys enjoy and let me know if you need anything else."

All three guys nodded in agreement. After Bennie had returned behind the counter and started waiting on another customer Bert said, "It's simply remarkable how

Bennie has turned his life around. Just about a year ago the only times we ever saw him was when we had to arrest him for being drunk. And then after getting that bogus job on Black Mountain it was like he hit a switch and turned his life completely around. It was too bad that company was not legit and he lost his job there, but ole Fred here was good enough to hire him. Fred you really did a good thing. Bennie's a new man."

"Sure is," replied Fred. "He's super reliable, very good with the customers, and as it turns out he's a lot smarter than people give him credit for being. He's a great Assistant Manager. I just hope he can stay off that booze, and so far, so good."

Bert and Kyle nodded agreement. Bert then said, "Guys, soon after I got in my office this morning I got a phone call that I need to tell you about. The call was from Max Snell, the Director of the Central Intelligence Agency. Mr. Snell said that his agency was well aware of our upcoming October Anchor Cross Festival, ACFesV. Because of the problems we've had in the past from North Korea he was concerned about security issues and expressed that his agency wanted to be helpful anyway possible. He's afraid Kim Jong-un may try something to disrupt the festival and possibly put many people's lives in jeopardy. As you know, he's tried several times in the past, and had any of those been successful many people could have lost their lives. He said his agency is getting chatter that indicates Kim might be up to something with the festival this year."

Fred and Kyle looked seriously at Bert. Fred said, "Did he say they knew anything specific?"

"No," answered Bert. "But he went on to say that he was going to assign two of his agents to Harlan from now until the festival to assist us with trying to uncover any unusual activity that could be related. He also said he had contacted our Governor, Bud Atherton, and suggested to him that the Kentucky National Guard should plan to deploy at least a couple dozen soldiers to help us with this year's festival security. Director Snell said the governor agreed and expressed his willingness to assist in any other way as well. Snell said he then requested that at least 6 Kentucky State Police officers also be assigned to the festival from Friday, October 2 through Sunday, October 4. Governor Atherton also agreed to this, saying he would reassign 4 of them from other posts, and only 2 from Harlan Post 10. The Director then said that we could therefore count on 30 additional security personnel, 24 from the National Guard and 6 from the State Police. He then said for us to work out the details of how these people would be deployed. I thanked him, and said we would do so. He then said he'd keep us posted on any future developments that his agency turned up."

"Wow," said Kyle. "Something must be happening for the Director of the CIA to be involved! That Kim Jong-un is a madman. No telling what he might be cooking up."

"Whatever it is, you can bet it's bad for us," said the mayor, "so now we've got something else to be worried and concerned about. We've got to protect the good citizens of Harlan."

The sheriff replied, "Well, the good news is it's just June and we've got some time to get all our ducks in a row before October. I just hope the Feds are able to find out more about what ole Kim is up to. It's hard to defend against the unknown."

Fred and Kyle each said, "Yeah." All three then silently drank their coffee and Kyle and Bert ate their doughnuts.

Kyle felt a rush of air off his right shoulder, and then felt Polly's feet resting there.

"Feed me, feed me," she begged.

Kyle smiled and broke off a portion of his doughnut and held it up in his right hand. Polly grabbed it and woofed it down in one quick swallow.

"Thank you. Thank you," the bird then said.

Fred swatted toward the bird as he said, "Polly, get out of here. No more mooching."

Polly quietly flew back to her perch and looked longingly toward the remaining doughnuts.

Fred then said, "Well guys, I guess we've got our work cut out."

Bert replied, "We do. I suggest as a first step we set up a conference call with the governor to talk about logistics. Maybe we could do that at 3 this afternoon in my office. Would that suit you?"

Both Fred and Kyle agreed.

Bert said, "Good. I'll have Rosie set it up with the governor's office. With this gloomy news I think we could use a little cheering up, Fred. What say you share something from your endless collection of funny stories?"

Fred though a minute, and then started, "There was a very famous Hollywood actor that made it a point to visit a nursing home regularly. He was always very fondly greeted by the residents. On this one trip the actor noticed that one man seated over in a corner didn't seem to recognize him. He walked over to the man and said, 'Hi there. Do you know who I am?' To which the man said, 'No, but you can go to the front desk and they'll tell you!' "

All three men roared with laughter as the two lawmen stood and headed toward their office across the street.

• • •

Same Day
Maggard's Grocery
Near Wallins, Ky.

"Good afternoon Mrs. Cavanaugh. I hope you were able to find everything you needed," Fatso said as he started to check-out her groceries.

"Yes, Fatso, I think I got everything. Thank you."

As he continued processing her groceries he said, "Mrs. Cavanaugh, I see here you're purchasing a can of beans. Do you know why they only put 239 beans in one can?"

Mrs. Cavanaugh got a smile on her face and replied, "Yes I do, Fatso. That's a very old one. They put only 239 beans in a can because if they put one more they'd be 240, and you always pronounce it as 'two farty'."

They each giggled, and then Fatso said, "I got a new one for you. What time is it when you have to go to the dentist?"

Mrs. Cavanaugh got a blank look on her face and said, "I really have no idea."

Fatso replied, "It's tooth-hurtie!"

Again they giggled. Fatso finished bagging the groceries and Mrs. Cavanaugh departed.

About an hour later Fatso was sitting on his chair at the check-out counter reading a magazine when Trigger Green came out of his back room office and said, "Fatso, I just had one of those strange phone calls from Pretty Boy Maggard. He said one of his clients wanted to send 10 people to Harlan and he needed our help. He said they wanted to buy the building in Harlan across the street from the Seibert Memorial to convert it to apartments. He wanted our help to arrange the sale and take care of all the particulars."

Fatso said, "You mean the building that for years was a drug store? The one catty-cornered from the Seibert Memorial on Central Street?"

"Yeah, that one," replied Trigger. "I told Pretty Boy we could probably arrange that, but why couldn't they do the deal themselves? He said they were foreign investors and their English wasn't too good and they didn't know all the ins and outs of our legal system. So I said, well, on the face of it it sounds like something that we could certainly do, provided, of course, our fee was sufficient. Then I about fell out of my chair when he said he would pay us $500,000 up front. We were to use that money to purchase the building and for the associated expenses, and we could keep any monies left over. In my head I quickly figured we could easily buy the property for $250,000, and there wouldn't be very many additional expenses.....so we could likely clear almost a quarter of a million dollars on this deal."

"Wow, that's a bundle! Gotta be something illegal going on for the bucks to be that big. What'd you tell him?"

"I thought about it. I didn't see how we could get in trouble just acting like a real estate agent. All we would be doing would be to arrange for the sale and then take care of all the paperwork to set it up. I agree with you that it smells, but for that kind of money I'm inclined to hold my nose and take it. So I told him to wire me the money."

Fatso replied, "So what's the next step?"

Trigger said, "Pretty Boy said the money would be in our account before the end of the day, and that we could expect the people to show up here at the store sometime in a couple of weeks. He said he knew there were already four apartments in the second floor of the building, and that the 10 of them would be staying there while they converted the ground floor and basement into apartments. So our purchase and any other work has to be completed within the next two weeks so they'll have a place to stay when they get here."

"Well, I know those 4 apartments on the second floor haven't been occupied in several years and are likely not in very good shape. We'll have to do a little work there to get them suitable for use. I assume they'll be completely renovating them too. But I feel sure we can accomplish that within a couple of weeks....especially for that kind of money," replied Fatso.

Trigger grinned and said, "I figured it that way too, Fatso. So we need to get started. You call the county clerk's office and see who owns that building and then try and set up an appointment for me with the owner asap."

Fatso said, "Will do, boss. But first you gotta tell me how you make Holy water."

Trigger turned and started walking back to his office.

Fatso yelled, "You boil the hell out of it!"

Chapter 2

5 months earlier, January
Pyongyang, North Korea

Chairman Kim Jong-un had many palaces in North Korea, but today he was in his office in the principal palace, located in the Capital city, Pyongyang. He sat at his desk staring at three military officers standing at attention in front of him. Each man held the rank of general, but each had different specialties. General Jung had a background in civilian and military building, similar in many ways to the U.S. Army Corps of Engineers. General Rhee was a specialist in explosives. General Yi had a conventional military background but had been assigned to Chairman Kim's intelligence gathering unit. All three men looked very uncomfortable standing before the Supreme Leader.

Kim finally said, "I don't have to tell you men how utterly disappointed I am over our recent attempts to steal those golden anchor crosses, and then having failed several attempts to extract revenge. Everything failed! Damn, Damn, Damn!" He pounded his fist on the desk and his face turned very red. "Our last mission, just this past Thanksgiving, was so close to perfection. And then some mangy pussycat did something at the last second to prevent our nuclear bomb from exploding! Damn, Damn, Damn. How much bad luck can we have?"

The three generals swallowed with difficulty, but none spoke. Their faces were turning very pale.

"But I'll tell you one thing, I will not tolerate failure. We will succeed. We will get those anchor crosses and we will get our revenge. Since that terrible Thanksgiving failure I've done nothing but think about a plan that will work.... and I've got one. And the three of you have been chosen to execute it. And to execute it perfectly. If you don't, then you will be executed. You understand that?"

All three nodded in unison and said "Yes Supreme Leader."

"General Jung," Kim said, "you will select five of your best men for the purpose of drilling a tunnel. I know your group has developed some very sophisticated drilling equipment and techniques that will be perfect for this mission. The first weekend in October each year the U.S. town of Harlan, Kentucky hosts a festival. It is called the Anchor Cross Festival, and celebrates the six mysterious artifacts that apparently have the power to protect from harm anyone possessing one. All six of these golden artifacts will be moved from a center at a university in Lexington, Kentucky to Harlan, Kentucky for this year's festival that starts on Friday, October 2nd. I have made arrangements for us to occupy a building that is located across the street from the Seibert Memorial that will house the artifacts for public display during the festival. The building we will occupy is currently vacant and we will occupy it under the pretense of converting the first floor and basement to apartments for rent and to renovate the existing apartments on the second floor. You and all your men will live in the existing second floor apartments. They will be made suitable for your use although they have been vacant for several years. This building also has a basement, and from this basement I want you to drill a tunnel under the street to the Seibert Memorial building. I want you to then drill upward and through the concrete floor, coming out exactly in the middle of the structure. This will permit us to steal the six anchor crosses during the night when the only guards are stationed outside the building. Do you understand, General Jung?"

"I do, Supreme Leader. I think I understand exactly. And we should be able to accomplish this with the use of our newly developed variable speed miner. As you know, it can dig a circular hole about two feet in diameter...large enough for men to crawl through. And since the speed of the drill is variable, when we get to the bottom of the concrete floor in the Memorial we will slow it down to a very slow speed that will cut through the concrete but will make very little noise. The guards stationed outside the building will not hear it."

"That's exactly what I had in mind," Kim said. "And when we get those golden anchor crosses we will be able to go anywhere we wish without fear of being stopped. They will be our ticket to world dominion. I'm already making plans for how we will use them." Kim's previously red face was now returning to normal, and even a slight smile formed.

"How long do you think it would take to drill the tunnel?" asked Kim

"Depending on the distance, but from your description I'd guess we could do the whole thing in a month to six weeks," answered General Jung.

"So if your team could be in place by the first of August you think for absolute certainty you could be ready to cut the hole in the floor of the Memorial on the night of Saturday, October 3rd?" asked the Supreme Leader.

"We can do it," replied General Jung.

Kim nodded approval, and then said, "General Rhee, I know with your extensive training in explosives you'll be perfect to accomplish our second objective. As I know you are aware, there are 10 deserters from our military that currently reside at a farm a few miles outside the town of Harlan, Kentucky. These 10 were sent to accomplish missions for me and failed. And then the sheriff of Harlan County took pity on them and arranged for them to receive political asylum and got them jobs at the farm. They are deserters! I want them dead! It will be your job to devise a scheme to accomplish that. And it should be done at the same time that the anchor crosses are stolen so as to not bring attention to our presence. Do you understand?"

General Rhee said, "I can certainly make that happen, Supreme Leader."

"Good, I thought you'd say that. I want you to select one other soldier to go with and assist you on the mission."

"Yes, Supreme Leader," Rhee replied.

"And then we have our third objective, General Yi. The sheriff of Harlan County has been central in all the efforts to thwart our previous missions. He must be eliminated. With your background in intelligence I thought you would be perfect to devise a plan to make him history. I'll also allow you to select one of your soldiers to go with and assist you in your mission. Okay?"

"Absolutely, Supreme Leader," replied General Yi. "It will be a pleasure to get our revenge. The sheriff's days are numbered."

"And his demise must also be arranged to take place about the same time as the other two missions, although it would be permissible for his death to happen several days before the festival just so long as we are not connected with it. I'm sure you could come up with something that would not link to us," said Kim.

"I can," replied the general.

Kim Jong-un pushed his chair back from the desk and stood up. He then said, "Generals, we have our plan. I'll expect each of you to gather all the information, tools, and equipment you'll need over the next 7 months and be ready to deploy to Kentucky in Late July. In the meantime we'll meet as I see the need. Feel free to phone me if you have questions. You are dismissed."

Each general saluted crisply, turned and exited. Kim smiled and sat down. He thought, *This time it's going to work. I'll possess those beautiful, golden anchor crosses and they'll be my ticket to dominating the world.*

•••

Monday, June 15, 3 pm
Harlan, Kentucky

The sheriff's office was crowded. Bert, Deputy Potter, Mayor Knapp, Pastor Raymond Bell and his wife Betty, and Harlan Police Chief Big Boy Asher, were gathered to participate in a conference phone call with Governor Atherton. In addition, Dr. Randy Peters from the Center for Appalachian Research at the University in Lexington was on the phone. Those in the room plus Dr. Peters consisted of the ACFesV planning committee, and sheriff Sterling felt the committee should all participate in the call to the governor.

Sheriff Sterling's phone rang. He picked it up and Rosie said, "Bert, the governor and Dr. Peters are on the line."

"Thanks Rosie," Bert replied as he punched the speaker phone button. "Good afternoon Governor Atherton and Dr. Peters." Each of the two replied with a cheery "Good Afternoon."

"I appreciate the two of you taking the time to chat with us. I've got our festival planning committee here in my office and my speaker phone turned on. I'll try and make this as short as possible, I know everyone is busy," said the sheriff.

"It is my pleasure to talk with each of you," said Governor Atherton. "I'm aware of the nature of our meeting, and it is certainly important. Anything my office can do to help is certainly offered. I just appreciate so much the excellent input from Sheriff Sterling, Mayor Knapp, and the rest of you. Please go right ahead Sheriff."

"Thanks Governor," replied the sheriff, "as I know you are aware, I received a call this morning from Max Snell, the CIA Director, and he was very concerned about more trouble from North Korea centered around our ACFesV. It's sure not every day I get a call from the CIA Director, so its caused a lot of concern for me and for the planning committee. We all feel that the Director would not have contacted us unless he felt pretty sure something was underway by that nutcase Kim Jong-un. I know you know all this, and I know he contacted you and you agreed to send us 24 national guard and 6 state police for the festival. I guess the main purpose of our call to you today is to ask if you know any other details you could share with us."

Governor Atherton replied, "All you say is true, Bert, and I can honestly say that I really don't know any more than that. Director Snell just told me what he told you, that the CIA had picked up a lot of chatter that seemed to be concerned with your October festival. Hopefully he'll be able to give us some additional information. In the meantime, how do you want me to set up the 30 folks to help with your security?"

"Thanks Governor," Bert said. "As you know, our festival always kicks off on Friday afternoon. So please have all 30 of them report to me here at my office around 9 am on Friday, October 2nd and we'll have figured out by then the best way to utilize them. In the meantime, if you hear anything further from Snell I'd sure appreciate your sharing it with us."

"Certainly I will," he replied, "and my best regards to the planning committee. One last thing let me add, I have reserved our state police helicopter for transporting Dr. Peters and the anchor crosses from Lexington to Harlan on the morning of October 2 and then to return them to Lexington late on the afternoon of Sunday, October 4th. Is that okay Randy?"

Dr. Randy Peters replied, "That'll work like a charm. Thanks for doing that Governor."

"My pleasure. And to everyone just again let me say that my office is prepared to assist in any way we possibly can. Just let me know if you think you need my help. It's been a pleasure talking with you."

"Thank you Governor Atherton. You take care, goodbye," Bert said.

"Goodbye," replied everyone else in the room along with Dr. Peters.

Two Days later
Wednesday, June 17
Washington, D.C.

The man exited along with all the other passengers on the flight from Atlanta to Washington's Ronald Reagan National Airport. He proceeded immediately to catch a cab, having no luggage to pick up, with only his carryon bag. The man was wearing casual clothes, tan slacks, a solid blue shirt, and a brown sports coat.

"Where to mister?" asked the cabbie as the man got in the back seat.

"CIA's George Bush Center at Langley," the man replied.

"Traffic's light, I should be able to get you there in about a half hour," the cab driver said.

The man was then quiet in thought as they traveled the George Washington Memorial Parkway North toward McLean, Virginia. They exited onto highway 123 and soon came to the entrance to the Central Intelligence Agency headquarters. About a mile later they arrived at the George Bush Center.

"Okay buddy, we're here," the cabbie shouted.

The man paid and thanked him, and began to walk up the stairs to the entrance. Upon entering he walked to the reception desk, pulled out his real passport, and said, "Good afternoon. My name is General Ri Pyong-rok from North Korea. I'm here to ask for asylum and to speak with Director Max Snell."

The somewhat stunned receptionist looked at the passport, and then said, "General Ri, if you would kindly be seated over there I'll contact our Director and someone from his office will be here shortly to accommodate you.

"Thank you," replied General Ri as he walked to a chair and seated himself.

In about 20 minutes two men in dark suits and ties came through a door in back of the reception desk and walked around to the general.

Dark suit #1 said, "You are North Korean General Ri?"

"Yes, and I would like to speak with your director," replied the general.

"Please follow us," dark suit #2 said as they began to walk back toward the door behind the reception desk.

General Ri was asked to first pass through a metal detector and then the two escorts asked if they could search him for any transmission equipment or other devices or substances he might be carrying. He agreed. After the search they then accompanied him down several corridors until they reached an office area designated as the directors. Inside the door there was a large room with half a dozen small offices and a receptionist in the center to which dark suit #1 said, "We have General Ri here for Director Snell."

The receptionist smiled, stood, and walked in front toward the door to the director's office.

Director Snell sat behind a large desk. He stood, walked around the desk, and extended his hand to General Ri. After handshakes, he said, "General, I must say this is truly an unexpected visit! Please be seated and let's talk."

They sat side by side on a sofa. General Ri said, "Director Snell, I'm honored that you would see me. I have an idea that your agency has files on me, but just let me say that I worked closely with Kim Jong-un to bring about the attempted nuclear bomb detonation over Harlan County, Kentucky last Thanksgiving. Being a prudent person, I had made arrangements to leave my country if anything went wrong with the Thanksgiving mission, labeled Project Bee Sting. I had the total responsibility for planning the mission. When I realized it had failed I immediately left North Korea. I knew the consequence of not leaving would be execution by Chairman Kim. Fortunately, I made it north out of Pyongyang to the border town of Dandong. I had a false passport identifying me as a Chinese citizen and exited Dandong into China. I traveled further north to the city of Shenyang, China where I have several friends. They took me in and I stayed with them until yesterday, when they drove me to Beijing where I boarded a plane destined to Paris. From Paris I flew to Atlanta, Georgia, and from Atlanta here to Washington. I have been traveling for the past 36 hours."

"Why did you leave China?" the director asked.

General Ri explained, "Around the first of the year I learned that Kim had found my two brothers and their families, and had executed them. I do not have any family left. I was never married, and my two brothers were all the family I had. When I got this word I started immediately to plan to come to the U.S. to ask for political asylum and to be of assistance any way I could to the United States. I realized what a terrible person Kim Jong-un is, and I'm very sorry to have followed him for so many years. My hope is that I can make it up in part by sharing my knowledge of him and his organization with you."

Director Snell reached across and patted the general on the back several times and said, "We will start the process for asylum immediately. You will be given new identification and papers. We will provide you shelter and living expenses. And in return, we would very much like to have detailed discussions with you regarding Kim Jong-un and your knowledge of his operation. Your appearance is so very timely. We have had indications that he is once again planning on some kind of mission pertaining to an October festival in Harlan, Kentucky."

"Yes, I am aware of that," replied General Ri. "I still am in contact with certain people that remain close to Kim but dislike him greatly. I do have some information regarding the mission you described."

Director Snell got a huge grin on his face and said, "Gneral Ri, let me get you taken to a nice hotel so you can get some very much needed rest, and then we'll get back together in a day or so to start your debriefing. How does that sound?"

The general nodded agreement and grinned. The two stood and shook hands.

Chapter 3

Monday, June 22
Maggard's Grocery
Near Wallins, KY.

Trigger Green stood beside the check-out counter talking with Fatso. He said, "Fatso, those 10 guys are likely to show up here about a week from now. Do you think we've done everything needed for them?"

Fatso replied, "Well, I think we're in good shape. Might be a few little details that'll come up, but all the big stuff's been taken care of. Mrs. Gilly was pleased as punch to sell that old drug store building for $200,000. That was 50 thousand less than we planned for...so that was good. I got the new deed all properly recorded in the name of

MIK Properties, just like you told me, with a Mr. Sammie Wong listed as the president."

"Okay, I'm sure that'll be fine," Trigger said, "I'm not sure how long they'll need to keep it. What about the apartments? What kind of shape are they in?"

Fatso said, "Actually, they weren't too bad. The people that had been renting them left em in pretty good shape. I hired a cleaning crew to come in and get em all fixed up. And then I got the utilities all turned on....so I think they're all set. I also got new locks put on the doors and got a dozen set of keys. That downstairs part, where the old drug store was located, is a real mess. And the basement's still got a lot of junk in it. But that'll be their responsibility, I guess."

Trigger said, "It will. So that sounds to me like we've done our part up to now. We'll just wait until the guys arrive and go from there."

Fatso said, "Tell me Trigger, why can't a bike stand on its own?"

Trigger just turned and started walking back toward his office.

Fatso shouted, "A bike can't stand on its own because it's two tired!"

Trigger chuckled and continued walking. He heard his cell phone ring and felt it vibrating in his pocket. He pulled it out, pushed the answer button, and said, "This is Trigger."

He stopped walking and just stood and listened for a couple of minutes. He then said, "Okay, I understand..... no problem. Everything's been taken care of and we'll see them then." He put the phone back in his pocket and turned and walked back to the check-out counter.

"Fatso, that call I just got was from Pretty Boy. He said the 10 guys would now not be arriving for about another month. I told him everything was all set whenever they got here. So I guess we just sit tight for a while."

"Makes no difference to me," replied Fatso. "But tell me why you never see hippopotamus hiding in trees?"

Trigger just stared at Fatso.

"Because they're really good at it," he said with a giggle

• • •

Same time
CIA Headquarters
Langley, Virginia

Max Snell sat behind his desk. General Ri was seated in a chair in front of the desk. The two had just received coffee. Max Snell said, "Well General, I hope you got some much needed rest this past weekend, and found your accommodations acceptable."

"I sure did, Director Snell, thanks so much for taking care of me. I feel much, much better this morning. Your people were very kind....even purchased me this new set of clothes and shoes. I really didn't have time to pack clothes. I truly appreciate it."

The director replied, "I'm happy you're happy! I wanted to bring you up to date on what we have planned for you. After we finish this meeting I have you all set up with several other agents to debrief you and gather any information you're willing to share with us. These meetings will take place for the rest of today and for tomorrow. You will continue to stay in the hotel until Wednesday morning. When you report in on Wednesday you will meet two gentlemen who will accompany you to Harlan, Kentucky. These two men are CIA Agent Cody Short and FBI Agent Sammy King. These two were previously assigned to Harlan during the Project Bee Sting operation. I got permission from the FBI director to again have the service of Sammy King since he and Cody Short are already familiar with Harlan, the people, and the surrounding areas. We all thought that we could best utilize your expertise by having you accompany them to Harlan. If Kim Jong-un is planning something there we think you might very well identify some of his people that might show up. Also we thought your other knowledge and contacts could best be utilized by your being there on the scene. But this is all subject to your approval, of course."

The general replied, "Yes, I understand, and I agree. Let me also say that I do know for a fact that Kim is planning an operation to both gain possession of the golden anchor crosses and to extract his revenge for the previously failed missions. Currently I don't know when this is planned to take place or other details. I just know it's in the works. I'm hopeful that I'll be able to get additional information from my contacts, and when and if that happens I'll certainly share it with you."

"You've made my day, General Ri. You are like a blessing sent from above! I truly appreciate your splendid cooperation. We'll take care of all the logistics of your trip to Harlan. We'll get you several sets of clothes, travel paraphernalia, etc. You and the two agents will have rooms at a nice Harlan bed and breakfast called the Harlan B&B. I'm sure you'll be comfortable there and I feel certain you'll greatly enjoy meeting the people in Harlan. My experience has been that they are super friendly and helpful."

"Thank you Director. Again, I feel really blessed."

Director Snell then excused General Ri to begin his debriefings.

● ● ●

Thursday, June 25
Harlan, KY.

Cody Short, Sammy King, and General Ri Kwang-choi were sitting at a large, round table covered with a white linen table cloth having breakfast at the Harlan B&B on South Main Street.

No other patrons were in the small dining room. The owner and server, Brenda Hider, asked, "Those clean plates tell me you guys liked your breakfast! Can I pour you more coffee?"

Cody Short smiled and said, "Sure Ms. Hider, that's mighty good coffee too."

Brenda filled all three cups to the brim and said, "Enjoy. Just shout out if you need anything else." She then turned and walked out of the dining room to the kitchen.

All three nodded approvingly. Sammy King then said, "Ri, you certainly do look different. I think our guys did a super job of changing your appearance. That long wig with the pony tail sure is different from your regular crew cut. And the fake mustache looks real as can be. And then the contact lens changed your eye color from brown to blue. It's just amazing how those three things completely changed your appearance. I bet your mother would have a hard time recognizing you!"

"But you must stop calling me Ri," the general said. "As you are well aware, my passport says my name is Joe Chang. Your people did an excellent job of replacing the old passport photo with the new one taken after my facial changes. And I thought it a good idea to keep my fake passport name of Joe Chang, since I'm accustomed now to being called that."

Sammy replied, "Absolutely, Joe, we'll be careful to not use your real name. From now on you are officially Mr. Joe Chang. Our first stop this morning will be over at the sheriff's office, and one thing I hope he'll be able to help us with is getting you a job here in Harlan. Everyone thought it would be best for you to be employed. We will still work together during your off hours, and on any occasion where you would be needed during business hours perhaps you could persuade your employer to allow you some time off."

"Yes, I agree," Joe replied. "And it would provide me some spending money as well. I don't want to keep requiring government financial support."

Cody Short looked a little sheepish and said, "Joe, before we go to the sheriff's office Sammy and I have to share a story with you. I know it will come up, and it's a bit embarrassing for us, but I think it would be better to tell you about it before we get there."

Joe looked a bit puzzled, and said, "Please do."

Cody continued, "Well, the sheriff's office has this mascot. She's a big, gray cat. Her name is Preacher Puss. She is a very, very unusual cat. One of her peculiarities has to do with pistols. She had some kind of bad experience in the past with a guy with a pistol, so now, anytime she sees one, she attacks the person possessing it. And I do mean attacks. She has claws you wouldn't believe, and she knows how to use em. Anyway, the first time Sammy and I visited the sheriff's office we didn't know about this. So when the cat's master, Deputy Rosie Cain, explained that the animal had gained a statewide reputation for subduing crooks when they flashed a pistol I made the mistake of pulling out my pistol and waving it around. Sure enough, the cat leaped onto my hand with the pistol and dug in those claws. Blood started spurting, I started screaming, and I dropped the gun. Unfortunately for Sammy, the gun fired when it hit the floor. The bullet went up Sammy's backside...and through one cheek of his derrière. In other words, he got shot in the ass. It was quite a scene. Sheriff Sterling had to take Sammy to the hospital, and my hand took over a week to heal. We were tremendously embarrassed at the time....and still are. Anyway, we thought we should share this story with you before we get there. So when you see Preacher Puss, and we'll let Rosie tell you the story about how she got the name, believe us when we say she's everything they'll tell you she is. She's even been made a honorary deputy sheriff. A remarkable creature!"

Joe couldn't suppress a grin. He said, "I'll bet that's the cat responsible for stopping the nuclear bomb explosion in Operation Bee Sting."

"Absolutely right," Sammy King said. "We'll let Deputy Cain or Sheriff Sterling tell you that story too, but you are certainly correct. Preacher Puss saved thousands of lives and put the quietus on Bee Sting. And that's not the first time she's done such a thing. Just a very, very strange and unusual cat. Let's go meet her!"

● ● ●

Deputy Rosie Cain heard the front door open. She looked up from her paper work behind the counter. Her face got a huge smile on it and she rushed around the counter, ran up to the three men, and hugged the two agents and patted their backs. She said, "Cody and Sammy, I thought I'd likely never see you two again after last Thanksgiving. But here you are! It's so good to see you once again. Bert said you'd be dropping by this morning. I just couldn't believe it." She then looked at Joe, stuck out her hand, and said, "I don't think I've had the pleasure of meeting you, sir."

Joe looked a bit embarrassed and said, "No, my first trip to Harlan. It is a great pleasure to meet you. Cody and Sammy have spoken very highly of you and the sheriff's office. My name is Joe Chang."

"A pleasure to meet you Mr. Chang," Rosie replied. "You guys have a seat here for a moment and I'll let Sheriff Sterling know you're here. He was on the phone a second ago, so it might be a few minutes." She walked back behind the counter.

"No problem," Cody said. The three took seats in chairs beside the wall.

There was suddenly a very loud "Meow". The three seated guys looked up and over Deputy Potter's desk at the shelf where Preacher Puss was intently staring down at them.

Rosie said, "Well, I'm sure Preacher Puss whishes to greet you three also."

The cat then jumped down to Deputy Potter's desk and from there onto the floor. She then walked over in front of the seated gentlemen. She first stopped in front of Agent Cody Short and allowed him to pet her and say, "Good to see you again Deputy Preacher Puss."

She then took a few steps and stopped in front of Agent Sammy King, who stroked her and said, "Morning Preacher Puss." The cat purred softly, then continued to walk in front of the seated Joe Chang. She then turned and jumped up into Joe's lap, laid down, gently purred and started slowly swishing her tail.

Joe smiled and started stroking Preacher Puss. He said, "I think she likes me."

Rosie said, "That's very unusual for her. She is normally pretty standoffish with people she doesn't know. It's as though she has identified you as a friend."

Joe replied to Rosie as he continued to pet the cat, "Well, that could well be. You see, I've been a bachelor all my life, and I've always been a cat lover. I previously lived in North Korea, and I had three cats....Winkin, Blinkin, and Nod. They provided me great companionship and comfort. When I had to suddenly leave my country last Thanksgiving I took the time to give the three cats to a very nice neighbor....so they still have a good home. Maybe Preacher Puss somehow senses that I'm a cat lover."

"Oh, how sweet," said Rosie. "I'm sure that's it. That cat has amazing instincts. I think you've already got another good friend."

Rosie looked at her phone console and said, "Okay guys, Bert's off his phone now. I'll let him know you're here." She stood and walked over to the sheriff's door, knocked, cracked the door and said, "Bert, you have three visitors."

The sheriff replied, "Please ask them to join me."

Joe gently placed Preacher Puss on the floor, and gave her a final nice long stroke. The three then stood and entered the sheriff's office.

"What a pleasure to see the three of you," Bert said as he shook hands with each of them. "Please have a seat and lets chat." Each was seated.

The sheriff continued, "I had a very unexpected phone call last Monday from Director Max Snell alerting me to some possible upcoming North Korea activity here in Harlan. He told me he would be sending a couple of agents to work with us, and then just yesterday phoned back with the really good news that General Ri, aka Joe Chang, had defected and would be accompanying you two. I was also just overjoyed to learn that the two agents he was sending were the two of you. Having worked on Project Bee Sting with us gives you a real heads-up on knowing people and places here in the county. Plus, you two were really good to work with. I'm just so glad to have all three of you here to help us."

Agent Short replied, "Bert, other than the unfortunate episode with Preacher Puss, Sammy and I thought our time spent with you last fall was very meaningful. You run a good office, and we're looking forward to trying to be helpful on this mission."

Bert grinned and said, "Speaking of Preacher Puss, does Joe know of your previous incident with her?"

Sammy responded, "Yes. We explained it to him this morning over breakfast. He's aware of how special that cat is, and that through our stupidity Cody got beat up pretty good and I got shot in the ass."

All four men laughed loudly. Joe then said, "Yes, that was quite a story. Preacher Puss and I got off to a good start this morning. I think she sensed that I'm a real cat lover, so she jumped into my lap and allowed me the pleasure of petting her. I think she and I will get along just fine."

Bert said, "Director Snell briefed me on the information the general shared with them. So I'm up to date on that. My understanding is that Joe confirmed the belief that Kim Jong-un is once again planning something to both steal the anchor crosses and to get revenge for his prior failed missions. Is that correct?"

Cody said, "That is exactly correct. And to answer your next anticipated question, we do not have any further information right now. That's about all we know."

Bert said, "Well, since he's again interested in stealing the anchor crosses, I would assume that the mission would be directed toward our Anchor Cross Festival in October. That's the only time the artifacts will be in Harlan, and I don't think he'd be stupid enough to try and grab them from Dr. Peters in Lexington. His Center has super security."

"Yes, that was exactly our thought as well," Sammy said. "But now we are fortunate to have Joe here, and he still maintains contact with folks close to Kim. Hopefully that will provide us with more information on what the Chairman is up to."

Joe then said, "Yes, but I do have to be very, very careful when contacting them. Should Kim have any suspicions at all, he would immediately have them executed. But we are lucky. There are two of these people and they secretly despise the Chairman. They will want to help us, but they know their lives are at stake. We have a prearranged plan to talk via secure satellite phones once a week. My last contact with them was last night, and they had nothing new to share then, but were overjoyed to learn of my new situation."

"Good to know," the sheriff replied. "I understand that the three of you are staying at the Harlan B&B. I'm sure Brenda will take good care of you."

"She has been super," said Cody. "We do have a request."

"Shoot," Bert replied.

"We would like for you to help us find a job for Joe. He would still work with us after hours, or even during work hours if requested, but we think it would be best for him to have a regular job. Our thought is that he would fit in much better that way."

"I understand," the sheriff said, "and I have a question for Joe. Do you cook?"

Joe laughed and said, "Cooking is my one hobby! I love to cook. What did you have in mind?"

Bert said, "By coincidence, I happen to know that our Chinese restaurant, called The China Pan, located just about a mile from the Harlan B&B is looking for a new cook. Their current cook is going to retire soon, and when I was there for a meal just a couple of days ago the owner, Mr. Lee, asked if I would keep my eyes open for anyone who would qualify. How's that for a coincidence? Not only is Joe a cook, but he's a Chang!! A perfect fit. What say you Chef Joe?"

"Divine interference," said a grinning Joe. "When could I start?"

"Well, I'll call them after our meeting and let you know....that okay?"

"Sounds really good Sheriff. I truly appreciate it."

"Good. So I'll let you guys go and get all settled. We'll stay in touch and get together again soon....except for you, Joe. You'll likely be cooking!"

All laughed and nodded in agreement as they stood and walked through the door into the reception room. Rosie said, "I trust you gents had a good meeting!"

Bert replied, "Yes we did, Rosie." All shook hands and as they approached the exit door each reached up to Preacher Puss's shelf where she was watching them and gave her a pet. When Joe reached up the cat emitted a loud meow and swished her tail briskly.

Chapter 4

Friday, June 26, 7 am
Harlan B&B
Harlan, KY.

"I just love the way you boys enjoy my food," Brenda said, "there's plenty more back there on the buffet....you just help yourself. Gotta have energy for a good day's work!." She filled the coffee cups of each of the three men.

"Mrs. Hider, you're going to spoil us," Agent Short said. "But we do appreciate it very much. Thanks."

"You're most welcome, honey," she replied. "By the way, I don't mean to be nosey, but are all three of you G-men? I remember from when Mr. Short and Mr. King stayed here back last November that they're G-men, and I know you all three arrived here at the same time, so I was just curious, Mr. Chang, if you're a G-man too?"

The three men laughed. Joe then replied, "No, Mrs. Hider, I just happened to arrive in the parking lot at the same time as my two new friends here, Cody and Sammy. We introduced ourselves there in the parking lot and have become good friends. I am starting a new job as cook at The China Pan on Monday."

"Oh, I see," she said. "I hope you don't think I'm being nosey, I was just curious. You'll like working at that restaurant. The guy that owns it, Mr. Lee, is very nice. I feel certain it'll work out well for you."

Joe replied, "Thanks, I'm very hopeful. And no, you weren't being nosey at all. We all three really are enjoying our stay here. You make us feel right at home."

"Well, thanks....I try. You boys have a good day," she said as she turned walking back into the kitchen.

Sammy said, "I'm glad we had our story all straight on that. And it worked out really good that Bert called last night to let us know he got you the job. I do feel it best if local people around town don't associate us together, Joe. I think that'll make both our jobs easier. I'm glad we drove here in two government cars, and that our guys were able to fix us up with Virginia license plates rather than U.S. government! Cody and I will make out fine with our one car and I'm sure yours will work for you."

"Oh, absolutely," replied Joe. "And I've got a nice Virginia driver's license to go with it! You CIA guys really have your act together!"

Cody said, "So, I guess our game plan will be for the two of us to work closely with Sheriff Sterling in trying to identify any unusual activity that might be coming from the Koreans, and you Joe will work at the restaurant each day and then spend time during off hours visiting about town to see if you might recognize anyone or pick up anything unusual that might seem to be pointed toward the festival."

Sammy and Joe both nodded affirmatively. "Joe then said, "Unless it's absolutely essential I won't be calling my contacts in Pyongyang except on Sundays. They expect my call on Sunday evening there, which is Sunday morning here. So I'll next be contacting them in a couple of days. I'll certainly let you know if there's anything new. Otherwise, I guess we just get caught up each morning here at breakfast."

"We're fortunate that Brenda operates this small B&B, and that she only has two more rooms other than our three.....and so far, they've been empty so we have this dining room all to ourselves. When she has other guests we'll have to be very careful not to be overheard if they're here in the dining room," Cody said.

The three finished their coffee with small talk.

•••

Same day, 9 am
Creech Cafe
Harlan, KY

Bert, Kyle, and Fred all sat huddled together at a table in the back of Creech's. Bennie had brought them coffee and Polly had been admonished by Fred to not dare bother them.

Bert said, "Our meeting and phone conversation last Monday with Governor Atherton went well. It was a good start. Too bad we're getting underway with all the ACFes planning with this North Korean thing hanging over our heads, but it certainly is good to at least know about it."

Fred replied, "Yeah, except that we really don't know about it. We just know that something's likely being planned. We've gotta know more than that to take some action."

Bert said, "But our ace in the hole is this fellow Joe Chang. He was a God-send. He knows Kim Jong-un as well as anyone, and he has contacts remaining there that are very close to Kim. I feel certain we'll learn what's being planned from Joe."

Kyle said, "Yeah, I sure was delighted to learn about him. He could certainly be the key to defusing anything they come up with."

"Are we 100% sure he's legit," Fred asked.

"He gets sent to us from the Director of the CIA
," Bert replied, "so I think we have to assume he's the
real deal. And we also have those two G-men. I sure thank
Director Snell for sending all three."

"Well, I feel pretty good about it. I think we'll get
information from Joe's contacts that will let us take care of
any threats they throw at us," Fred said.

The three sipped their coffee in thought. Kyle said,
"Bert and I better be heading over to the office. Care to
send us off with a smile, Fred?"

Fred got a sparkle in his eyes, reached into his shirt
pocket, pulled out a newspaper clipping, and said, "I just
happened to see this one in yesterday's Harlan Enterprise
and was getting ready to tape it up on one of my walls.
I'll summarize it for you. There was this elderly gentleman
named George who was living his last days in a nursing
home. One day George was sitting in a chair looking very
sad. Nurse Curnin walked up to him and asked if there was
something wrong. He replied that his private part had died,
and he was very sad. The nurse, knowing that the patients
were sometimes a little crazy, told him to please accept her
condolences. The next day George was spotted by Nurse
Curnin walking down the corridor with his private part
hanging out of his pajamas. She ran up to him, shook her
finger in his face, and told him to please put his private

part back inside his pajamas. But George then told Nurse Curnin that he had told her yesterday his private part had died. She acknowledged that, but then wanted to know why it was out of his pajamas. He replied that it had died yesterday and today was the viewing!"

Bert and Kyle were still laughing when they got to their offices.

• • •

Monday June 29, 9 am
Sheriff's Office
Harlan, KY

The ACFesV planning committee was once again assembled in the sheriff's office. In addition to the sheriff and deputy Kyle Potter there were the committee Chairman and Harlan Mayor Fred Knapp, Pastor Raymond Bell and his wife Betty, and Harlan police Chief Big Boy Asher. The other member, Dr. Randy Peters, would join the meeting via speaker-phone. Gunsmoke Slusher had also been invited by the sheriff. The seven sat in front of Bert's desk sipping coffee and chit-chatting.

Mayor Knapp then spoke toward the speaker phone, "Randy....are you there?"

"Sure am Mayor. I hear you loud and clear!"

"Great. All the rest of the planning committee are here in Bert's office, and we also have Gunsmoke Slusher as a guest this morning," Fred said.

Everyone shouted a 'Hi' to Randy, and then the mayor said, "First off I think we should go over everyone's responsibilities and make sure those are clear, and then Bert want's to share some recent information he got yesterday afternoon. It pertains to security, so we'll hold that topic until last."

The committee proceeded to discuss who had what responsibility for contacting all the people who would be involved in the festival. All the musicians, the speakers, the concessionaires, the publicity, parking and traffic control, finances, etc. were all discussed. The agenda for the three days was also covered. They then turned to the last topic of the meeting, security.

"Okay Bert, you want to share with the folks the new information you got yesterday afternoon," the Mayor said.

"Thanks Fred," Bert replied. "Each of you know that CIA Director Snell alerted us about a week ago about possible North Korean activity associated with this year's festival. He didn't at the time have anything specific, just that there was a lot of chatter coming from Pyongyang that seemed to relate to ACFesV. He told me that he would be sending us two agents to work with us, and they have, in fact, arrived. They are the same two, Cody Short and Sammy King, who were here last fall and helped us with Project Bee Sting. Director Snell also sent a third person, Joe Chang, that has contacts in Kim Jong-un's office. Mr. Chang now works as a cook at The China Pan, but he'll be here to also assist us any way he can. Please do keep this information strictly confidential. I received a phone call from him yesterday afternoon saying that he had phoned his contacts yesterday morning and had learned that Kim had given orders for the preparation of false documents, including passports and Indiana driver's licenses, for 10 of his military. And apparently remarks were made regarding these documents that they were important for the Chairman's getting revenge for previously failed missions in Harlan County. And it's for that reason that I invited Gunsmoke Slusher to sit in on our meeting today. As you are all aware, Gunsmoke and Booger now employ ten ex-North Korean soldiers that were previously involved in failed missions here that were ordered by Kim. So I think that those ten could well be targets in whatever it is that Kim might be planning regarding his revenge. We really don't know anything further at this time, but Gunsmoke, I think I'd start to think about maybe added security at your farm, and also informing all the guys about the possible attack and that they should be really alert to any suspicious activity."

Gunsmoke answered, "That's real good information to know, Bert. Thanks for sharing it. I'll certainly talk with all my folks and make sure they're extra vigilant. That nutcase Kim has certainly been a big problem for us, but we'll do everything we can to keep him from harming anyone. Please do let me know if you find out anything new about his plans."

"You know I will, Gunsmoke," the sheriff said. "Chief Asher, Kyle, and I will be working on all the security plans for our festival. Just one last comment, I do wonder why the 10 soldiers are being given Indiana driver's license? Let's all give that a little thought. It might be a key to identifying them. I think that's about it for our meeting. Any comments by anyone?"

All nodded agreement and as everyone stood getting ready to depart Mayor Knapp said, "Thanks for hosting our meeting, Bert. And thanks to each of you for attending..... and Dr. Peters, thank you for tuning in!"

Randy replied, "I heard all that. Thanks, and you all take care."

The last two to leave the meeting were Gunsmoke and Bert. As Bert walked Gunsmoke to the front door the two looked up at Preacher Puss's shelf and saw the cat looking intently at them. Gunsmoke reached up, stroked her, and said, "Preacher Puss....you'll always be Smoky to me! I'm so proud of the job you're doing here in the sheriff's office. I'll give your regards to Booger and all the others at the farm.....especially to all the other cats!"

Preacher Puss purred loudly, stood up, and swished her tail. Bert reached up and gave her a nice pet as Gunsmoke walked out the door.

Chapter 5

Monday, July 27
Pyongyang, North Korea

The Supreme Leader actually had a pleasant look on his face. The three generals, Jung, Rhee, and Yi stood at attention before his desk. He said, "Generals, the time has come for execution of our new mission. I've decided to call it Project Gold Rush. Each of you have been busy over the previous months preparing for it. All of you and your chosen soldiers will leave tomorrow for the U.S. I want assurance from each of you that everything is in order. General Jung, please report."

Jung replied, "Yes Supreme Leader, everything I'm responsible for is ready to go. I have selected 5 very capable and devoted soldiers to accompany me. We have all our equipment selected and packed ready for transport. The largest item is the portable variable speed miner which weighs about 300 pounds and is packed in a wooden crate."

Kim said, "Good. General Rhee."

"Yes Supreme Leader, all is set with me and my selected soldier. We have been studying the Slusher Farm where the 10 deserters now live and have come up with a plan to eliminate them. I have coordinated everything with generals Jung and Yi, and I believe our plan is sound."

"Good, General Yi."

"I have been studying extensively all the files and information I could find about Sheriff J. Bert Sterling. I have selected one soldier to accompany me, and we have developed two schemes for eliminating Sheriff Sterling. If the first fails, then we have a backup. All is in order, and we look forward to leaving tomorrow to accomplish our mission."

"Good. Then the three of you along with the 7 selected soldiers will leave Pyongyang tomorrow morning. You will fly via our private jet to Havana, Cuba. Mr. Maggard has, according to my directions, arranged for the captain of a fishing boat to meet you at the airport. Bribes have been paid to airport personnel to permit landing and unloading there. The boat is called Island Time and it's captain is named Juan. He will meet you at the airport with a van large enough to transport all men and cargo to his boat. You will then depart Cuba and travel up the Atlantic coast of the U.S. to the city of Brunswick, Georgia. You will be met at the Brunswick marina by a fellow named Sonny who has been hired by Mr. Maggard to deliver to you a car and a passenger van. The van will be large enough to accommodate 5 men plus all the equipment and luggage. Five men will travel in the car. From Brunswick you will travel to Knoxville, Tennessee where you will meet Mr. Maggard. He will have accommodations where you will stay for two nights to get rested prior to proceeding to Harlan, Kentucky. If all goes as planned, and it damn well better, then you should arrive in Harlan on Saturday, August 1. Is this clear to everyone?"

The three generals nodded affirmatively and said in unison, "Yes Supreme Leader."

Kim said, "To celebrate our upcoming successful mission, I have a special treat for you."

He then punched the intercom button on his desk and said, "We're ready for the food. Bring it in."

An aid then opened the door and pushed a cart with food into the room. He handed each general a large mug filled with soup and a spoon. Onto the Supreme Leader's desk he placed 3 Big Macs, 2 large fries, and a chocolate and a vanilla milk shake. The aid then turned and left.

Kim had gotten very fond of McDonald's food when he was a student studying in Switzerland. After becoming Supreme Leader he sent a team of chefs to Switzerland for a month to learn how to make all the entrees on the McDonalds menu. They each gained 12 pounds while on this assignment, but were successful in being able to reproduce all the menu items.

Kim said, "Generals, you each have a very special soup I had prepared for you. Eat up."

While continuing to stand at attention each general started eating their soup. Each formed a frown on their face, but continued to eat until their bowls were empty. By the time they finished and placed their bowls back on the food cart Kim had polished off all the Big Macs and fries and was finishing up the second milk shake.

Kim then said, "I'm sure each of you remember General Ri Pyong-rok. He was responsible for the execution of Project Bee Sting. As you are aware, that mission failed. General Ri evidently had made preparations to flee our country if this occurred. We know that he left and entered China at Dandong, but couldn't track him from there. We did, however, discover that his neighbor was a close friend. When we visited at their home we discovered that General Ri had left his three cats in their care. First we executed the neighbor and his family. Then we tortured and killed the three cats. We had learned their names were Winkin, Blinkin, and Nod. General Jung, the soup you just ate was Winkin soup, General Rhee had Blinkin soup, and it was Nod soup for General Yi. I wanted each of you to be reinforced as to what will happen to your families, pets, and those close to you if you fail in this mission. Do you understand?"

Each general looked green and as though they might throw up. They each swallowed and said in unison, "Yes Supreme Leader."

"Although we couldn't locate General Ri after he fled, my guess is that he went to the U.S. and in all likelihood is now in Harlan County, Kentucky. If you happen to locate him during your mission please kill him for me. The one who does that will be greatly rewarded."

Kim continued, "All papers and clothing have been assembled for the ten of you. Satellite cell phones are in the packages for each of you generals and I expect you to keep me informed daily on your progress. Do you understand?"

All nodded and said, "We do, Supreme Leader."

"Then go forth and accomplish Project Gold Rush."

Each general saluted sharply, turned, and walked out of the office.

Kim Jong-un grinned and thought, *In about two months I'll be the most powerful man in the world. I'll be able to use those golden anchor crosses to make other nations bow to me. Whatever is my desire will be within my grasp.*

● ● ●

Same Day
Lexington, Kentucky

Dr. Randy Peters, Director of the University of Kentucky's Center for Appalachian Research, sat in his office with a visitor, CIA Director Max Snell. The two had been served coffee after Dr. Peters had taken Director Snell on a tour of the Center.

Max Snell said, "Randy, your operation here is most impressive. I'm still in awe from looking at those unbelievable golden artifacts. Just to see them and think about their history is mind boggling. I'm also very impressed by the security you have here. I think anyone breaking in here and stealing those anchor crosses would have to be good enough to break into Fort Knox."

Randy laughed and said, "We do try to make sure they're safe. After all, they're not even ours. They belong to owners around the world, and we sure appreciate their letting us keep them here for research and study."

"I understand," the CIA Director replied. "And it's the question of security that brings me here today."

"I sort of thought that might be the purpose of your visit," replied Randy with a smile.

Director Snell continued, "You are well aware that the festival in Harlan is coming up in October, and, being on the festival committee, you know that we've received some possible threats from North Korea that seem to be aimed at ACFesV."

Randy nodded in agreement.

Max continued, "The fact that those artifacts seem to possess unbelievable power has been a great concern for my office for many years now. We are well aware of the potential threat they could have for our country if any foreign power could get their hands on them."

Randy interrupted Max and said, "Possibly. But you do understand that as far as we've been able to establish their power can only be used to bring about peaceful and good results. We've found no instance where they served an evil purpose."

"Yes, I do understand that," Max replied, "but as far as their security is concerned, anyone attempting to steal them would likely not know, or at least not think, that they would not accomplish their evil goals. They would be blinded by the thought that if they possessed them they could use them to accomplish any and all of their evil desires."

Dr. Peters nodded and said, "Yeah, I can certainly see that."

"So after having had many meetings discussing this," Max said, "we want to recommend something to you that on first consideration you might well not agree with. But we'd like you to give our recommendation some thought, and then if you agree we'll proceed to make it happen."

Randy looked intrigued. He said, "You bet, anything you guys think best will certainly get my utmost attention. What exactly do you recommend?"

"Okay," Director Snell replied, "Here's what we would like to do. My office has assembled a group of the very best craftsmen they could identify to work exclusively to accomplish this project in the next six weeks. There are eight of these craftsmen, and they are standing by in a fully equipped workshop awaiting our word to get started. If you approve, they will make six anchor crosses identical in looks to your originals. Every detail will be exact. The only difference in composition will be that the fakes will be made by gold plating over copper cast anchor crosses. To look at the fakes no one would be able to tell them from the real thing. And even to lift and carefully observe them would pass muster. That they were fake could only be determined by digging into them to find their core is copper, not pure gold. We did give thought to using pure gold for them, but then realized that wouldn't be necessary to accomplish the goal we have in mind. And that goal is to have the fakes rather than the originals on display at ACFesV. We believe that if North Korea tries anything at the festival it will be to steal those anchor crosses. And even though security there is good, we'd like to make absolutely sure that those precious artifacts could not fall into their hands."

Randy then said, "I understand your plan and the reason for it. The only problem I have with it is that we would then be deceiving the people who came to the festival to view the genuine anchor crosses. That I have a problem with."

Max said, "Yes, I do understand, but I would ask that you think of what could possibly happen if the real artifacts fell into enemy hands. And we too had thought about your concern. I would suggest that if you elect to allow us to proceed to make the duplicates that they be kept a secret from everyone. Only the two of us would know the fake anchor crosses were made. I can assure you that the craftsmen that would make them are bound to secrecy. So then all the others on the ACFesV committee could in truth represent the artifacts as the real thing. And should you be asked about them, I'm sure you could reply in a way that simply didn't state that those in Harlan were fakes. I would not ask you to lie."

Randy thought about that for a couple of minutes and then said, "Okay, Max. If you think that the best course of action, I'll go along with it. I know you need to get the craftsmen started to allow them time to complete their work in six weeks. How can I help?"

"They'll need to visit here first in order to carefully observe the artifacts, take photographs, dimensions, weights, etc. They can be here tomorrow if you give me the okay."

"I'll make arrangements for them to have exclusive access tomorrow afternoon. When they arrive just have them ask for me and I'll cook up a story to tell my secretary so she won't know who they are. Then they can stay as long as they wish, even into the evening if need be. Is that suitable?"

"Absolutely," Director Snell said. "I'll call and have the arrangements made immediately.

After his phone call the two men chatted for another few minutes and then Max Snell left for Blue Grass Field and his flight back to D.C.

•••

Tuesday, July 28, 11 pm
Jose Marti International Airport
Havana, Cuba

Captain Juan stood beside the large van he had borrowed from a friend. After the bribes had been paid to the general aviation personnel, he was allowed to drive the van onto the airport property to await the arrival of the North Koreans' private jet. He smoked a cigarette as he waited next to the area where he was told the jet would be parked. Everything was very dark and very quiet. After smoking the one cigarette and then half way through another he first heard, and then saw the landing lights, of a plane approaching a runway. The sleek jet landed and proceeded toward Juan. He stomped out his cigarette and waved a flashlight toward the approaching plane. It parked exactly where Juan had been told it would. Shortly after the engines were turned off the passenger door on the side of the plane opened and the steps extended down. A parade of ten men then exited the plane. The first was General Jung. He extended his hand to Juan and said, "I presume you are Captain Juan. My name is Jung. So glad to see you here as planned."

Juan replied, "My pleasure. Let's get your luggage and cargo loaded in the van and we can be off to my boat."

General Jung nodded approval and all the Koreans accompanied Juan to the rear cargo door on the jet. It had been opened and luggage started being handed down, and then all the cargo, including the 300 pound crate that contained the miner. After getting everything loaded in the van, the flight crew in the jet closed all the doors and began moving toward the runway for takeoff back to Pyongyang, and Juan began the drive to his boat at the Havana marina, a distance of about 20 miles.

They arrived at the Island Time shortly after midnight. After moving all the cargo onto the boat the Captain's mate removed the mooring lines and they started their journey to Brunswick, Georgia. The Island Time is a semi-displacement hulled boat and travels at just over 20 knots, so the approximately 500 mile trip from Havana to Brunswick would take about 24 hours. All the Koreans were very tired and went below and either found a bunk or made one on the floor and were asleep almost immediately. Captain Juan and his one mate stayed at the helm during the journey

•••

Thursday, July 30, 2 am
In the Atlantic
Off Brunswick, Georgia

Generals Jung and Yi emerged from the cabin and walked over to Captain Juan at the helm. The captain smiled and said, "Gentlemen, I trust you had a restful night." He pointed toward the land on the western horizon and continued, "We are just about 10 miles off Brunswick. Should be at the marina in less than an hour."

Both generals grunted. General Yi said, "I think about half our crew are seasick, but they'll recover quickly. Speaking for myself, I did get a little more sleep, after sleeping until about noon yesterday. How about you, Jung, did you get some shut-eye?"

General Jung nodded and said, "Yeah, a little. But I'll sure be glad to be on dry land again."

Captain Juan laughed and said, "Well, just hang in there. We'll dock before you know it."

In about 30 minutes the Island Time passed between St. Simons Island on her starboard and Jekyll Island on port. Captain Juan said to the two Koreans watching his progress, "We're just about now at the exact location where that large cargo ship carrying South Korean cars overturned a few years ago. They just recently completed salvage operations and got the channel all cleared up."

The generals just grunted. Captain Juan then made a port turn and proceeded under the huge bridge that connected Brunswick with Jekyll Island and then turned to starboard and entered the Turtle River. About a mile further they arrived at the Brunswick Landing Marina, located only a couple of blocks from downtown Brunswick. It was 3 am. Juan saw a flashlight waving from a slip on one of the marina's piers. He slowly moved the Island Time into the slip.

Juan's mate threw the boat's lines to the fellow with the flashlight who secured them to the dock's cleats. They had arrived.

The captain jumped off his boat beside the flashlight guy. "Hey! I'll bet you're Sonny."

"Yep, you got that right. You run a good ship, captain. You're almost exactly on time."

Juan looked down the pier toward the parking lot and saw a large passenger van and a car parked beside it. A guy was getting out of the van and walking toward the pier and the boat."

Sonny said, "That's my buddy coming there with the hand cart. He'll help us get everything unloaded and into the van."

General Rhee and the other Koreans came up out of the cabin carrying their luggage and cargo. After everything was stowed in the van Sonny reached into his pocket, pulled out a cell phone, and called for another friend to come pick the two of them up at the marina.

Captain Juan extended his hand to General Jung and said, "Mission accomplished. At least my part! Good luck to you guys, where ever you're headed."

Jung shook hands with Juan and said, "Thanks captain. You have a safe trip back to Havana."

Juan and his mate walked back to their boat, cast off the lines, backed the boat out of the slip, and faded into the night on their return trip.

Sonny handed Jung the keys to the car and van and said, "Good to do business with you guys. Everything's all paid for. Both vehicles have Indiana license plates, and false papers in the glove compartment. My advice would be to not break any laws and not get stopped by the cops. If they checked those papers they'd find they're bogus.'

Jung took the keys. He saw another car pull up next to the van. The general said, "I guess that's your ride, Sonny. Appreciate your help. You rest assured we'll drive very carefully and not break any laws."

Sonny and his buddy got in the car that had just arrived and it sped off.

Five of the Koreans were assigned the van by General Jung. The other five, including Jung, got in the car with Jung at the wheel. He took a minute to set up the electronic GPS map system in the car, setting its destination as Maggard's Junk Yard in Knoxville, Tennessee. Following its directions, he pulled out of the marina parking lot with the van following close behind. He turned left (north) on highway 25 and after a couple of miles came to Interstate 95. They turned north on the interstate headed for Tennessee.

Chapter 6

Thursday, July 30th, 4 am
Along Interstate 95
In South Carolina

General Jung's car, followed by the van, pulled into a rest area to use the facilities. All ten men marched into the welcome center and then into the rest room.

At the same time a unit of the South Carolina National Guard pulled into the rest area. They were headed to Fort Brag, North Carolina for their two week summer training session. There were about a dozen army vehicles, everything from jeeps to large cargo trucks. 24 soldiers, dressed in military fatigues, got out of their vehicles and headed toward the rest rooms.

The Koreans had assembled together in the welcome center after finishing in the rest room. General Jung said, "Okay guys, it's time to hit the road again." He started to lead the procession out the door when he looked up and saw a line of military vehicles parked outside and a couple dozen military soldiers walking toward them. "Quick, back in the rest rooms....everybody get in a stall and lock the doors." The ten turned and quickly ran into the men's room. Fortunately, at this early hour of the morning they were the only occupants. Each one ran to a stall, went in, locked the door, and sat down on the toilet. That left only 4 empty stalls.

The officer in charge of the National Guard unit, a Colonel Hayes, led his men into the welcome center and then toward the men's room. Most went to the urinals, but 6 needed to take a dump. 4 found empty stalls, but two had to wait. Those two stood outside the long row of stalls and noticed feet under all 14 stalls. After about 5 minutes one of the National Guard soldiers exited his stall and one of the waiting two entered it. The remaining Guardsman standing in wait thought it a bit strange that no one had come out any of the other stalls. After another couple of minutes the door opened on one of the stalls used by a fellow Guardsman, and after he exited the last waiting Guardsman entered the stall. After another 5 or so minutes, having relieved himself he exited the stall and started to walk back into the welcome center. Just before doing so, however, he again glanced and noticed that 10 stalls were still occupied. And since he'd not heard anyone leave or enter while doing his business, he assumed the same 10 must still be in those stalls. He shrugged, and then walked into the welcome center to join his fellow Guardsmen.

Colonel Hayes said, "Private, we've been waiting here almost 15 minutes for you. You have a problem?"

The private replied, "No sir. I just had to wait for an empty stall. There were a total of 14 of them, but they were all occupied. Sure was a strange thing, the last 10 in the row remained occupied the whole time I was in there."

The Colonel said, "Well, we got better things to do than to analyze how long people take to crap. Let's get underway." All the Guardsmen then followed the Colonel to their vehicles and left the rest area.

General Jung's stall door slowly cracked open. He saw no one and came out. He said loudly, "Okay men, listen up. I'm going to look out into the welcome center to see if the soldiers have left. Each of you stay in your stall until I come back." After exiting the men's room and looking carefully around he saw no soldiers and noticed that all the military vehicles had left. He went back into the men's room and said, "All is clear. Come out, and let's hit the road."

• • •

Same Day, 9 am
Harlan, Kentucky

Sheriff Sterling, Deputy Potter, and Mayor Knapp were once again gathered around a table in the back of Creech Cafe having their morning coffee. The sheriff said, "Guys, everything sure has been quiet over the past few weeks. Nobody has noticed anything unusual going on, and I've not heard anything new. The two G-men have been busy checking around, and Joe Chang's not reported anything new. I get a little uneasy when things are this quiet."

Kyle and Fred nodded. Fred said, "Well, the good news is that all the planning for the festival seems to be going well. Everyone's doing their job. But I'll sure feel better when I know for sure there won't be any nasty business from those North Koreans."

Bert replied, "That's exactly how I feel too, Fred. And I keep checking with the Slusher brothers and they say everything seems fine on their end. Nothing new. All the Koreans there are doing great and haven't been contacted by anyone."

Kyle said, "I have the feeling that we'll learn something soon. The festival's only about two months off now, so if there are bad things in the works they'll likely start to show."

Fred and Bert nodded agreement.

Bert said, "Well, I guess we just keep on keeping on."

Kyle replied, "Yeah, but I bet ole Fred here could give us something to smile about before we get started for the day."

Fred pointed to a newspaper clipping taped on one of the store's walls and said, "I just put that one up there yesterday. It's about an elderly couple that were seated and eating in a fast food restaurant. They had ordered one hamburger, one order of fries, and one soft drink. The gentleman had carefully cut the hamburger in half, divided the fries evenly, and poured half the soft drink into another cup. Those sitting around them noticed this and thought that the couple couldn't afford to buy food for them both. A man walked over to their table and asked if he could be permitted to buy them another meal. To which the lady replied that they were fine, they just liked to share everything. The gentleman then proceeded to eat his half of the hamburger, his half of the fries, and to drink his half of the soft drink. Another man saw this and walked over and asked if he could buy them a meal.

The gentleman said that was a kind offer, but that they just always shared everything. As the man walked back to his table the gentleman looked at his wife, reached up and pulled out his teeth, handed them to his wife and said it was her turn!"

Bert pounded the table as he laughed, stood up, and said, "Thanks Fred, that'll keep us smiling until at least noon. The lawmen walked out of Creech's toward the Court House.

• • •

Same Day, 10 am
Maggard's Grocery
Near Wallins, KY.

Fatso sat sound asleep in his chair at the checkout counter. Trigger walked up from his office and slammed his fist down hard on the counter. Startled, Fatso jumped up, passing gas loudly, and said, "Trigger, I sure hope you enjoy doing that. I don't know how much more my poor heart's going to take of that nonsense."

"Something smells bad," Trigger said as he grinned. "You gotta quit sleeping on the job, Fatso."

"Yeah, yeah. Like I got a lot to do," Fatso replied. "So what's going on?"

Trigger replied, "I just had another call from Pretty Boy wanting to tell us that the guys that'll be moving into the old drug store building should get here Saturday around noon. He wanted to know if we have everything all set for them. And he wanted to know if we got the carpenters hired to assist with the renovation starting on Monday. I told him that all is good to go. You did get those carpenters all hired, didn't you?"

"Sure did," replied Fatso. "When we got his request last week I immediately contacted Sunshine Fix-It. Those brothers Bob and Bud Rehsa can do about anything. I thought they'd certainly be up to helping with that renovation. They agreed to the $75 per hour for the two of them, and said they'd report there at 8 am on Monday morning. Just like we planned."

"Sounds fine," Trigger said. "The money don't bother me....that'll be on the other guys to pay em. I just wanted to make sure we had it set up, which was our responsibility to Pretty Boy."

Fatso said, "Yeah, I know. We're all set. Tell me Trigger, where do you find elephants?"

Trigger shook his head and said, "You watch for those guys to show up here around noon on Saturday." He then turned and started walking back to his office.

Fatso grinned and shouted, "You find elephants where you left them."

Trigger slammed his door shut.

● ● ●

Same Day, 3 pm
Maggard's Junk Yard
Knoxville, Tennessee

Pretty Boy Maggard sat in his dilapidated old chair with his feet up on his trashy desk. He was in the office building of his junk yard. From where he sat he could see through a large window in the front of the office toward the junk yard entrance where the gate stood open. He saw a car followed closely by a passenger van entering his property. He jumped to his feet and ran out to meet them.

The two vehicles stopped in front of the office and slowly 10 men emerged. Pretty Boy threw open his arms and said, "Welcome, welcome, welcome. I've been expecting you guys. I hope you had an uneventful trip."

General Jung stepped forward, smiled, and offered his hand to Pretty Boy. As the two shook hands he said, "My name is Jung, and I assume you are Mr. Maggard." Pretty Boy nodded in agreement. "And yes, for the most part we did have an uneventful trip, other than one small incident in a South Carolina rest area. But all's well that end's well....and here we are. I understand you have accommodations for us for a couple of nights, and then on Saturday morning we'll be off to Harlan, Kentucky. I was told that you would give us directions as to how to make contact there and where to go."

"Jung, you exactly right!" Pretty Boy replied. "I know you boys have had a long and hard trip, so I've got you all fixed up at a good motel just about a block from here. There's a good restaurant right beside the motel, and I think you'll be able to get plenty of rest and good food starting shortly. After I take you there and get you all checked in you can come back here on Saturday morning and I'll give you all the information you need to get to Harlan and to your place of business there. That sound okay?"

All ten Koreans smiled and nodded in agreement.

Pretty Boy said, "Super. I'll jump in my pickem up truck and you just follow me.

The three vehicles exited the junk yard.

Chapter 7

Saturday, August 1
Maggard's Grocery
Near Wallins, KY.

Fatso looked at his watch. It showed 12:30 pm. He thought, *those guys from MIK Properties were suppose to get here around noon. It's after noon and not a sign of em*. He returned to reading his magazine. Fifteen minutes later he saw a car and a van pull into the parking lot. Both vehicles had Indiana tags. He punched his intercom button and spoke to Trigger, "Hey, I think our guys are here. You better come out to meet them."

Trigger replied, "Be right there." His office door opened and he came walking briskly toward the store's front door.

In the parking lot General Jung opened his car door and stepped out. He looked toward the front of the store and saw Trigger coming out toward him. He waved, smiled, and said, "I'll bet you are Mr. Green."

"Folks call me Trigger," he said as the two of them shook hands. Trigger looked at the car with four other guys in it, and then over to the van and figured it had about the same number. He then said, "Come on in and we'll get you the information you need. Don't your guys need to get out and stretch their legs or go to the john?"

Jung replied, "No, we stopped in Pineville for gas and they got all taken care of. I think they're fine. As soon as I can get the information from you on the property and the keys we'll head there and get all settled in."

The two walked back into the grocery store.

Fatso yelled, "Hi there guy. I'm Fatso. Welcome to Harlan County!"

Jung looked a bit surprised, then said, "Thank you Mr. Fatso. My name is Jung. It's good to get here."

"Hope your trip from Indiana wasn't too bad," Fatso said. "Tell me Mr. Jung. Do you know the difference between a mouse and an elephant?"

General Jung looked puzzled. He said, "Well, I know one's large and one's small."

Fatso laughed and said, "Close. But no cigar. The

difference between a mouse and an elephant is about one ton!"

Trigger looked at Jung and said, "Pay no attention to Fatso. He just likes to tell corny jokes. Let's go to my office." The two walked through the grocery and into Trigger's office.

After being seated Trigger said, "I've been in contact with Mr. Maggard regarding the needs for you and your crew. We have purchased the building and property located at the corner of 1st and Central Streets in Harlan. And as you requested, it's purchased in the name of MIK Properties LLC of Indianapolis, Indiana. Fatso had a cleaning crew come in and clean the upstairs apartments and got all the utilities turned on for you. Those apartments aren't in the best of shape, but should be suitable for your temporary living quarters until you get them renovated. The ground level, which previously was a drug store, is in pretty bad shape, as is the basement. So I guess you have your work cut out to make all the changes. Also, Fatso hired two really good handy men to assist you, as was also requested by Mr. Maggard. The handyman company is called Sunshine Fix-It. It's owned by a couple of brothers. Their names are Bob and Bud Rehsa. You will pay them $75 per hour, and they have been told to start on Monday morning at 8 am."

Jung nodded approval.

Trigger then handed Jung a box containing 10 keys. Fatso had gotten a dozen, but Trigger kept two just in case they needed to get in there for any reason. He also gave Jung a business card with his cell phone number, and a sheet of paper with a map showing the location and address of the property. Trigger then said, "Mr. Jung I think this should get you going. Fatso also stocked one of the refrigerators with food to get you started. You think of anything else we can do for you?"

Jung looked over everything, then said, "I think this will do it. My car's GPS will get me to the property address, and if we have additional questions or need anything else I'll give you a call, Mr. Green. You have been very helpful. Thanks so much."

The two stood, shook hands, and Trigger started walking Jung back through the grocery to the parking lot. Fatso shouted, "Hey Mr. Jung, You know what you call an elephant in a phone booth?"

Jung grinned but kept walking behind Trigger toward the door.

"You call the elephant stuck!" shouted Fatso with a chuckle.

"Ha Ha, Mr. Fatso," the general replied. "That's a good one. And thanks so much for your help in getting us all set up in the property."

"No problem, Mr. Jung. You just let me know if I can help further."

The two walked out the front door, Trigger again shook hands with Jung, and watched as he got in his car and the two vehicles departed headed toward Harlan.

Trigger then walked back in the store and over to the check-out counter. He said to Fatso, "That went well. Everything seemed in order. What'd you think?"

Fatso replied, "Yeah, but maybe a little too smooth. You know that Jung and those other fellows with him all look a lot like the Koreans that we previously got involved with on several different occasions. And they were all up to no good. You think we could have a problem again?"

"I hope not, Fatso. But I agree with you, they do look similar to the Koreans we've previously dealt with. But I guess we have to give them the benefit of the doubt..... especially since we're being paid so handsomely by Pretty Boy."

"Yeah, that bothers me too," Fatso replied. "With that much money something surely doesn't smell right."

"We'll watch it closely." Trigger replied.

Fatso nodded and said, "Trigger, you know what you get when you cross an elephant and a computer?"

Trigger shook his head and started walking back to his office.

Fatso smiled and said, "You get a 2 ton know it all!"

The door to Trigger's office slammed shut.

•••

Fifteen minutes later General Jung turned his car off the Harlan By-Pass onto Mound Street. Followed closely by the van they proceeded to 1st Street, turned right, past the Harlan Post Office on the right and then as they approached Central Street Jung was relieved to see that beside their property on the right side there was a loading zone large enough for both his car and the van. They both parked there.

General Yi had been driving the van. He and General Jung met as the others started to get out of the vehicles. General Jung said, "Yi, we were fortunate that there was this loading zone. I was worried about how far off we might have to park. This is perfect. We're right beside the property."

Yi nodded in agreement and said, "Yes, I too was concerned. That miner weighs about 300 pounds. And some of our other equipment is very heavy as well. Maybe it would be a good idea to go inside and look around to see where we should put everything before we start unloading."

Jung said, "Yes, I agree. I've got 10 keys here. I'm

going to pass one to each of you guys. Guard it carefully." He then gave each of the other 9 a key.

With the three generals in the lead the ten walked into the old drug store and surveyed the three levels. They then unloaded all the cargo, taking it to the basement, and their personal luggage and other items to the apartments upstairs. All the equipment placed in the basement was boxed securely in unmarked wooden crates. All the soldiers started unloading their suitcases and getting settled in their apartments except for General Jung. He walked back downstairs and outside to lock their two vehicles. After locking the car he was walking to the back of the van to make sure the rear cargo doors were locked. Walking down Central Street toward him was Bennie Sekao. Bennie was taking his afternoon break from work at Creech Cafe, and had decided to get a little exercise by walking around the block. He had exited the restaurant, turned left and walked to 2nd Street, turned left up 2nd to Mound, left again on Mound to 1st Street, and then after crossing the street he turned left again on 1st, past the post office, and then encountered the person locking the vehicles.

Being the outgoing person that he was, Bennie stuck out his hand to General Jung and said, "Hi there. My names Bennie Sekao. I don't believe I've seen you here in Harlan before. Are you new here?"

Jung was surprised, but shook hands with Bennie and said, "Yes, My name is Jung. I work for a company in Indianapolis. The company bought this property and we just arrived and are getting moved in. We are going to convert the entire building into apartments."

"Oh, that sounds exciting," Bennie said. "I work at Creech Cafe just about a half block up Central Street from here. We've got pretty good food. You and your men come check us out."

Jung replied, "That's good to know Mr. Sekao. We certainly will."

Bennie smiled and continued walking to Central Street where he turned left across 1st and continued toward Creech's. The general finished locking everything up and returned to his apartment.

• • •

Monday, August 3
Creech Cafe
Harlan, Kentucky

Deputy Kyle Potter had to make a run to a reported home burglary first thing this morning so only Sheriff Sterling and Mayor Knapp were huddled together at a table in the back of Creech's. Fred, with a smile and a chuckle, said, "Bert, I was just listening to radio WHLN interviewing a physician on the subject of senility. The doctor said one good thing about being senile is that you can hide your own Easter Eggs."

Bert laughed, took a sip of coffee, and said, "Well, I guess there's a positive side to everything!"

Fred replied, "Yeah, I guess. Say, Bert, have you heard anything new at all from our friend Joe Chang or the two G-Men?"

"Nothing at all," the sheriff replied. "And everything still seems very quiet in town."

Bennie walked up with the coffee pot and said, "You guys ready for another shot of mud?"

Both men nodded. Bennie started pouring their coffee and said, "While I was out for a stroll on Saturday I ran into a guy beside the old drug store building there at the corner of 1st and Central. He was locking a van and getting ready to go in the building. I introduced myself and found out that he's with an Indianapolis company that bought the building and is going to restore it to all apartments."

Both men looked with interest toward Bennie. Fred said, "You said he told you he was from Indianapolis......as in Indiana?"

Bennie looked puzzled and replied, "Yeah, that's what he said. And I noticed the van and a passenger car parked in front of it both had Indiana tags."

Bert said, "What did this guy look like?"

"Well, that was kinda interesting," Bennie said, "he looked foreign. As a matter of fact, he looked for the world a lot like our Korean friends that live at the Slusher farm."

Bert looked at Fred and said, "Things just might not be so quiet after all!"

Bennie looked perplexed. He said, "Anything wrong? I hope I didn't do something bad?"

"No, no, Bennie, as a matter of fact you did real good," replied the sheriff. "It could well be nothing, but what you just told us could possibly be a lead on an investigation we have ongoing. Please don't say anything about our interest in them. It's important that they not know. You understand?"

"Oh sure Bert, I understand. My lips are sealed," said Bennie. He walked away to another table.

Fred whispered to Bert, "What'd you think?"

"Could just be a coincidence, Fred, but the fact that they have Indiana tags and that there's a bunch of them and they look Korean certainly sounds suspicious to me. Joe Chang's information said that Kim was having 10 Indiana driver's licenses and passports prepared. It's certainly something I'm going to check out. As a matter of fact, I'm going over there right now and see what I can learn."

Fred said, "Be careful my friend."

Bert stood and said, "Always, my friend!" He hurriedly walked out Creech Cafe, took a right on Central Street, and began thinking about what he would say to the newcomers.

Bert got to the front door of the old drug store and knocked. After only a few seconds the door opened and there stood Bud Rehsa. Bud said, "Well as I live and breathe, I do believe I'm looking at Harlan's finest!"

Bert, shaking hands with Bud, said, "Well, I don't know about that 'finest' business. Good to see you Bud. You and Bob working on this apartment job?"

"Sure are Bert," Bud said as the two turned and walked inside the first floor.

Bob Rehsa dropped a crowbar and rushed over to join his brother in greeting the sheriff. "Hey Bert, so good to see you. I hope your presence here doesn't mean anything's wrong."

Bert laughed, shook Bob's hand and said, "No, no. Nothing's wrong. Bennie Sekao just told me that he had met one of the guys as he was moving in on Saturday, and I just wanted to drop by to say hi."

"Yeah, all the guys are upstairs now. I'll go get Mr. Jung and let you meet him. Bud and I were very pleased to sign a contract with this company....it's called MIK Properties. They're going to put apartments in the basement and here on the first floor, and then we're going to renovate the upstairs apartments. Should be a good job for Sunshine Fix-It! I'll go get Jung," Bob said.

Bud and Bert continued to chat while Bob climbed the stairs to retrieve Mr. Jung. In just a couple of minutes the two returned downstairs.

Jung looked slightly pale as he saw the uniformed sheriff. He extended his hand and said, "My name is Jung."

Bert shook hands and said, "Mr. Jung my name is J. Bert Sterling. I'm sheriff of Harlan County. Folks just call me Bert. Please do."

"Thank you Mr. Bert," replied Jung. "I hope there's nothing wrong."

"No, no. As I just told Bob I was having coffee this morning at Creech Cafe and the Assistant Manager there, Mr. Bennie Sekao, told me he met you Saturday as you were arriving. I just wanted to drop by to say hello, and wanted you to know that the sheriff's department would be pleased to be of service should you need us."

"Thank you Mr. Sheriff," Jung said. "I think we're okay right now."

"One thing I was wondering, Mr. Jung. I haven't been here in this old drug store for many years. Would you mind just showing me the basement and upstairs, and to give me a little more information about your company. I just might be able to recommend you to some friends looking for an apartment."

"Certainly, Mr. Sheriff. Please follow me." Jung and the sheriff turned to walk toward the door going down into the basement. Bert said to Bud and Bob, "See you guys shortly. You can get back to work."

Jung opened the door to the basement, turned on the lights, and the two men descended the stairs. Jung said, "As you can see, we just moved some of our equipment and parts down here in the wooden crates. Everything else is pretty much junk that we'll be getting rid of."

Bert replied, "Yeah. Looks like there's enough room down here for a couple of apartments."

"That is our plan," Jung replied. They walked about the basement and then back up the stairs and to the upstairs apartments. They entered each of the four apartments. As they did the Koreans all stood at attention beside their beds. After the sheriff was introduced to everyone they walked back down to the first floor.

"You have a big job here Mr. Jung," Bert said. "I wondered about your company. I see your vehicles have Indiana license plates. Where are you from?"

"Our company is MIK Properties, LLC, headquartered in Indianapolis, Indiana," Jung said as he handed the sheriff a business card. "The head of our company, a Mr. Wong, is Chinese, as are we. Mr. Wong came to this country about ten years ago and started the company in Indianapolis. He has a childhood friend that lives in that city and the friend finally talked Mr. Wong into moving there. He was very successful, and through his contacts in China he recruited fellow countrymen to come join him. I and the 9 others here are the results of his recruitment. We refurbish old buildings into apartments. This is our first such job in Kentucky. "

Bert looked at the business card and said, "I see. Well, your cell phone number is on here. So if I have any need to contact you I'll give you a call. I appreciate very much meeting you and thanks for showing me around."

"You are very welcome, Mr. Sheriff. It was good to meet you. I'm sure our paths will cross again."

Bert shook hands again with Mr. Jung and turned to walk to the front door.

Bob and Bud yelled "See you Bert. You come back and visit!"

"Sure will guys. Don't work too hard."

Bert left the building, crossed the street, and walked toward his office. He thought, *Those guys appear legit. But all the facts we got from Joe Chang fit them exactly. 10 people, Indiana driver's license, and all Asian. I'm gonna check out this MIK Properties and Mr. Wong when I get to the office.*

Chapter 8

Tuesday, August 4
Creech Cafe
Harlan, Kentucky

Head for the hills, head for the hills," Polly squawked as Bert and Kyle walked into Creech's. Both men reached up and gave Polly a nice pet. Kyle said, "You stay put bird." They then headed toward their table at the back of the cafe.

Bennie shouted, "Be right there with the coffee, boys."

"Thanks Bennie," Bert replied as they took their seats.

Fred saw them through the window in his office and came out and joined them. As he sat he said, "Morning guys. Bert, I've sure been curious what you found out in your visit to the old drug store yesterday morning."

Bennie arrived, poured three coffees and said, "Let me know if you need anything else guys."

All three smiled and nodded to him. Bert then said, "Yeah, I'm sorry I didn't get back with you yesterday Fred, but it got a little busy for me. When I arrived there yesterday morning I was greeted by Bud and Bob Rehsa. They were hired by this MIK Properties company to help with the apartment conversion. I then met with a Mr. Jung. He seemed to be their leader. He showed me all around and introduced me to his coworkers. There were 9 of them.....so 10 including Jung. Everything looked very legit. There were lots of crates in the basement and the upstairs apartments were occupied by the personnel. The downstairs, the old drug store part, looked pretty bad but the Rehsa's were already underway working on it. Jung told me that the company was out of Indianapolis. The founder, a Chinaman named Mr. Wong, lived there and had used his contacts in China to recruit all the workers."

Fred said, "Well, sounds like you think it legit."

"Yeah," Bert replied, "It sure appeared to be. But since everything matched the information we had been given by Joe Chang I felt I needed to check a little further into the company. So when I got back to the office I got on my computer and started checking it out. Sure enough, there is a MIK Properties in Indianapolis owned by a Mr. Sammie Wong. The company address and residential address for Mr. Wong are the same. But that's not unusual, I guess he has an office on his property. So that seemed to check out."

Fred said, "Umm, so you really think them legit?"

"I don't know what to think for sure," Bert replied. "I just have a hard time discounting the coincidence of Joe Chang's information matching exactly. But the fact that Bud and Bob are there working with them certainly seems to further indicate they're for real. Right now I don't know what to do other than keep an eye on them and maybe check in occasionally with the Rehsa brothers. I feel absolutely confident that they would not knowingly be involved in anything illegal. What do you guys think?"

Kyle said, "I guess that's about all we can do right now."

Fred said, "Well, in addition to checking with Bud and Bob maybe ole Bennie could drop in on them occasionally. He did meet Jung, and the Rehsa brothers are good friends."

"That's a good idea Fred," the sheriff said. "I certainly can't take any action at this point. I just don't have any evidence that they're not who they say they are. But my gut feeling is that they are the 10 guys Joe Chang indicated might be coming here. And speaking of Chang, maybe we could arrange something where he could see one or more of them to see if he recognizes them. We'd have to be careful....they might recognize him and blow the whole thing."

Kyle said, "Yeah, we could do that. I think we should give it some thought. Also, maybe we need to share what we know about MIK Properties with the two G-Men. It wouldn't hurt to have them watching their operation as well."

"Yeah, I'd had that thought too," Bert replied. "I think I'll set up a meeting with the G-men and Joe just to bring them all up to date."

Fred and Kyle nodded agreement. All sipped their coffee.

Bert finally said, "Kyle and I better get back across the street. Fred, you have anything new to make us smile?"

Fred immediately pointed to a newspaper article taped to the wall above their heads. He said, "Put that one up just this morning. It's about a preacher delivering a sermon on forgiveness. At the end of his sermon he asked if everyone would be willing to forgive all their enemies. About half the congregation held up their hands. Not pleased, the preacher continued the sermon for another

10 minutes and then repeated the question. This time, since Sunday lunch was on everyone's mind, all raised their hand except one little old lady. The preacher asked the lady to come forward. After getting to the front the preacher asked her why she was not willing to forgive her enemies. She said because she didn't have any. The preacher replied by saying that was very unusual, and asked if she knew why that was . She said sure, at age 94 she had outlived them all!"

Kyle laughed and said, "Well, that's one sure way not to have enemies. We should be so lucky!"

Kyle and Bert stood with smiles. Kyle said, "Thanks Fred. That'll hold us for a while."

•••

Same Day, 8 pm
The Old Drug Store Building
Harlan, Kentucky

General Jung had gathered all of the North Koreans around a makeshift table on the main floor. He said, "Okay guys, we've put off getting underway with our three missions long enough. We've got the Rehsa brothers well underway working on this floor. It'll keep them busy until we finish our missions and are gone. As you know, I told them that we would be working on the two apartments in the basement as well as refurbishing the upstairs apartments. So they have no business coming to either of those locations. But as a precaution, be sure to lock your apartment doors when you are not in them, and we'll keep the door going to the basement locked at all times. We'll tell the brothers to knock if they need us for any reason. Let me just go over our plans for the basement one final time. It needs to look like we're installing two apartments down there, just in case that sheriff or some other person shows up with a valid reason for looking. So we're going to first install a back wall for the apartments that will run the entire width of the basement. It will be set out 6 feet from the actual basement back wall. That will be our secret work area. The width of the basement is about 30 feet, making the secret work area 6 X 30. That should be sufficient. We'll then build all the other walls for the two apartments but have a passage door in the back wall of the west apartment. If anyone asks, we'll say it's a service door to the utility panels and plumbing. Is that clear?"

All nodded that they understood.

Jung continued, "So, first thing in the morning we move all of our equipment crates to the back wall. We've already gotten rid of most of the junk in the basement, and we'll have to next finish that job. Once we have the basement all cleared out we'll be ready to begin building the false apartment back wall and then the other walls as per our plans. Once we get that back wall finished we won't be in any hurry to complete the rest of the apartments. We'll then be able to unpack the variable speed miner and drill a hole through the back wall. As those of you on my team are well aware, we have the exact coordinates for the middle of the Seibert Memorial across the street. So once we drill the hole out of the basement we'll begin drilling the hole under the street. We've checked out all the utilities that could be a problem and know that we should be fine at the depth we're drilling the hole. Once we drill to the position directly below the center of the Memorial Building we'll turn and drill upward until we hit the concrete slab floor. When we do that we'll have to wait until Saturday night, October 3rd. After the Memorial is closed for the night we'll begin the process of drilling through the concrete floor. We will slow the drill down until it's at a very slow speed in order to make minimum noise. My understanding is that there will be no guards inside the building. They will be stationed just outside. The noise from our slow drilling should not be a problem. Once through the floor we'll gather the 6 golden anchor crosses, take them back through our tunnel, and then be on our way back to Pyongyang. Any questions?"

One of the 5 members of Jung's group said, "General Jung, Do you think we will have enough space to store the dirt we remove?"

Jung said, "As you know, that was a major concern. But we will have enough room. Our 6 foot by 30 foot area should easily hold the dirt we remove to make the two foot diameter tunnel. The biggest problem we'll have is the slow dirt removal. We have no automated conveyor. The removal has to be by hand. I'll be purchasing two children's wagons to use for carrying the dirt. We'll simply have to operate the miner for a while, stop it, pull it back out of the tunnel, and then hand load the dirt it has produced into one of the wagons and pull it out and dump it in our 6X30 foot space. We'll need to pile the dirt up to the ceiling. It'll be slow going, but all that was figured into the time we have to complete our mission. We should have no problem arriving at the bottom of the Seibert Memorial floor by October 3."

General Jung then said, "General Rhee, are you all set with your mission to eliminate the 10 deserters?"

Rhee responded, "We are working on our plans. We will be putting all the details together and certainly will be ready to execute it at the festival."

"And General Yi, your mission is to eliminate Sheriff Sterling. Everything looking okay there?" asked Jung.

"Yes. As you know, we have two plans. A primary and a backup. We will be evaluating when to execute our mission over the next week or so. Everything looks favorable," said Yi.

Jung continued, "Congratulations gentlemen. I think the Supreme Leader will be very pleased when I convey this information to him. One thing more I'll mention is that the visit from Sheriff Sterling, while unanticipated, worked out to our advantage. He toured our building and found everything to be as advertised. And I feel sure he checked out Sammy Wong in Indianapolis. We are indeed fortunate that Supreme Leader Kim had contracted with Mr. Wong about 8 years ago to set up MIK Properties. That company has served our country very well, and the fact that it had been an established corporation for 8 years surely satisfied Sheriff Sterling completely. I reported this to our Supreme Leader this morning and he laughed and said that Sammie Wong had been a vital connection for us on many occasions. He was pleased with our progress. Okay, our meeting is adjourned. Get a good night's rest, we have a very busy day tomorrow."

•••

Wednesday, August 5, 3 pm
Pyongyang, North Korea

Supreme Leader Kim Jong-un was sitting at his desk having his afternoon snack. He had just polished off two Big Macs and two chocolate milk shakes. He didn't have any fries....he was trying to cut back. He was expecting a satellite phone call from General Jung. It was 6:00 am in Kentucky, and the generals usually called daily about this time.

His satellite cell phone rang. "Go ahead," Kim spoke into it. He listened as General Jung brought him up to date on the progress and the meeting they had last night.

Kim said, "Excellent. So everything seems to be going very well. Two months from today you and all our soldiers should be back here in Pyongyang. I'll have the 6 golden anchor crosses and the 10 deserters and Sheriff Sterling will all be history. Thank you General Jung. Give my regards to the others. That will be all for today."

After disconnecting the call Kim sat back in his chair with a very satisfied look. He thought, *I do believe that this time we will succeed. How fortunate it was that Sheriff Sterling decided to drop by and pay a visit to the old drug store. And we were so lucky to have set up the story about MIK Properties with my long time good friend Sammie Wong in Indianapolis. I have paid Sammie hundreds of thousands of dollars over the past 8 years, but it has paid many dividends.* He chuckled and thought, *And that name, MIK Properties. I bet no one has ever discovered that MIK is Kim spelled backwards! I thought that was a very nice added touch by Sammie.*

● ● ●

Thursday, August 6, 8 am
Sheriff's Office
Harlan, Kentucky

Bert sat at his desk. Cody Short, Sammy King, Joe Chang and Deputy Kyle Potter sat in front of the sheriff's desk. Bert had just thanked the guys for attending at such an early hour, and explained that it was necessary so that Joe would not miss any work. Bert then briefed the G-Men and Joe Chang about the 10 Asian fellows in the old drug store building, and what transpired when he visited there on Monday.

"Well, that explains one thing," Joe Chang said. "Late Tuesday afternoon we got an order phoned in for 10 dinners. Then when a guy named Jung showed to pick them up, I saw him from the kitchen. He did look familiar, but I couldn't place him at the time. Now, from what you've just said Sheriff Sterling, I think the fellow could well have been in the North Korean military. I saw someone that looked like him on several occasions when Kim held meetings with military personnel. But I did not know his name."

Deputy Potter sat up straight in his chair. Bert got a very satisfied look on his face and said, "Okay. That is very good information to have. Although the group seems to have covered themselves with a false company in Indiana, the information you got previously from your contacts plus this possible identification of Jung sure seems to make it at least an 80% probability that these are the bad guys."

The two G-Men and Kyle Potter all nodded vigorously.

Kyle said, "So what's our next step?"

"Certainly not enough evidence to shut them down," Bert replied. "I suggest that Joe try to arrange something where he could see some of the other 9 guys, and hopefully be able to identify them. And Cody and Sammy could maybe focus on them as well. We really don't know what they're up to, and we certainly need to find out."

Sheriff Sterling's intercom buzzed and Rosie said, "Sorry to interrupt, Bert, but Carolyn is on line 1."

Bert seemed to blush a tad and said, "I'll have to take this guys. I told Rosie to always put Carolyn Potter through to me if she called."

Deputy Kyle Potter, Carolyn's son, blushed a bit as well. He and the other three gentlemen smiled and nodded approval. Carolyn and Bert had been friends since high school, and had dated regularly for many years. They usually set aside Thursday evenings as date nights, and most every Sunday attended church together followed by lunch.

Bert picked up the hand receiver, punched 1 on the phone set, and said, "Hi Carolyn, I hope everything is fine." He then listened and kept nodding his head. "Okay, that sounds great, I'll see you there at 6 o'clock. You take care."

With a sheepish grin he said, "Sorry guys. It was just Carolyn wanting to know if I would like to have dinner this evening at The China Pan. Knowing they have a very good cook, I told her yes!"

Joe Chang smiled and said, "I'll make sure we have something real special on the menu tonight!"

After a bit more small-talk the group broke up. As the G-Men and Joe walked out the entrance door they each looked up to acknowledge Preacher Puss. Joe was first in line. The cat stood up and seemed to anxiously await receiving a pet from him. He obliged. She gently swished her tail and meowed. Cody and Sammy just saluted as they exited. Sammy was last out and said, "Keep everything under control Preacher Puss." She watched them closely as they went out. She then made one 360 degree circle around her shelf-bed, and then gently and slowly lowered herself again in a curl. Her head was pointed directly toward Rosie Cain behind the counter. Rosie laughed when Preacher Puss appeared to wink at her before closing both eyes and continuing her nap.

• • •

Same Day, 6 pm
The China Pan Restaurant
Harlan, Kentucky

Bert looked at his watch and frowned. Carolyn was once again running late. He had arrived at The China Pan about 10 minutes ago and gotten seated. He was on his second glass of iced tea.

Joe Chang came rushing up to his table and said, "Sheriff, we just got another take-out call from the same guy at the old drug store. He ordered 10 dinners again. Said the ones they got Tuesday were so good everyone wanted to order again. He or someone from his group should be here shortly to pick up the order. I thought you'd want to know."

"Yes, thank you Joe. Better make yourself scarce, but hopefully you'll be able to see the guy when he picks up the order," Bert replied.

"Yes," Joe said as he turned and started back toward the kitchen.

The front door opened and Carolyn Potter strolled in. She saw Bert, and headed toward his table. Once seated she said, "Sorry I'm a few minutes late. I couldn't find my car keys."

Bert smiled and said, "Haven't heard that one for a while!"

Carolyn smiled, reached across the table, patted Bert's hand and said, "Now, now. It happens to be the truth!. How was your day?"

Bert briefed her on his day, including the meeting that morning with the G-Men, Joe Chang, and her son Kyle.

She again reached across the table, stroked his hand, and said, "Honey, those North Koreans have come very close to killing you several times in the past. I'm really worried that this could present a whole new threat to you. Are you concerned?"

"Of course I am," Bert replied. He reached down with his other hand and patted hers. "But I'm sure it'll be fine. Preacher Puss will watch out for me."

They both laughed. The entrance door opened again and in walked General Rhee. Bert said to Carolyn, "Excuse me just one second."

He stood, walked over beside Rhee at the counter, offered his hand and said, "I don't recall your name but I think we met last Monday when Mr. Jung was showing me around at the old drug store."

Rhee stiffened, shook hands with the sheriff, tried to grin and said, "Yes, Mr. Sheriff, you are correct. So good to see you once again. I came to get dinners for all our crew. This place has very good food."

"It does indeed," Bert replied. He pointed toward Carolyn and said, "My friend and I were just getting ready to order. I just wanted to say hello. Enjoy your meal, and tell everyone hello for me."

"Yes, I certainly will," replied Rhee.

Mr. Lee walked up to the counter and handed Rhee three large bags containing his food order. He said, "That order comes to $83."

Rhee pulled out a hundred dollar bill, handed it to Mr. Lee, and said, "I don't need any change. Thank you." He then grabbed the bags, turned and nodded toward Bert as he walked out of the restaurant.

Carolyn asked, "Was that one of the guys you were talking about?"

"It was," Bert replied. "They say they are from China, so I guess they like Chinese food!"

Mr. Lee walked over to their table and took their order. After about 5 minutes Joe Chang came back out from the kitchen and asked Bert if the fellow was one of those he saw earlier in the week at the old drug store.

"Yes," Bert replied. And after introducing Carolyn said, "Did he look familiar to you?"

"He did, but again I don't have a name. His face looked like someone I have seen before, but not often. Just about the same as with the other fellow from there."

"Okay," the sheriff replied. "Keep your eyes and ears open."

"I certainly will," Joe said as he turned and walked back to the kitchen.

Chapter 9

Friday, September 18
Creech Cafe
Harlan, Kentucky

Fred spoke, "Guys, it's now only two weeks until our festival. Amazingly, all the planning seems to be going perfectly. As you know, the committee met just last Tuesday and not a single member reported any problems with their assigned responsibilities. So, all is well as far as I can determine regarding the program and activities. But this thing with the North Koreans is worrying me to death. Is there nothing new on that front?"

Fred, Bert, and Kyle were once again huddled at their table at Creech's having morning coffee.

Bert replied, "Fred, I wish I had something better to tell you, but nothing new has developed now for several weeks. Joe Chang has spent many, many hours parked in his car outside the old drug store trying to catch a glimpse of those guys. He thinks he's likely seen all of them now at one time or another, but he can only report that three of them look somewhat familiar....and he doesn't have names for them. So, not much there we can act on."

Kyle said, "I bet the poor guy sure gets tired of sitting in his car."

"I'm sure he does," Bert said. "I'm just glad none of the MIK guys have recognized him. I guess his wig with the pony tail and mustache have been enough to keep him from being identified. And all that car sitting is done after work hours and on weekends. He sure hasn't had much of a life. But he's certainly devoted to helping us. I don't think I told you about his latest contact from Pyongyang. When he phoned there last week he was told that some of the people in Kim's office were laughing about the soup that had been served to three generals a month or so earlier. Apparently the soup had been made from cats that had belonged to Joe and given to a neighbor when he left the country. So Joe learned that not only had his beloved cats been killed by Kim, but very likely the neighbor and his family as well. "

"Boy, that's sad," Fred replied.

"Sure is," Kyle said, "but at least we know he's really devoted to helping us prevent Kim from causing more trouble."

Bert and Fred nodded. Fred then said, "And there's nothing new on what those MIK guys might be up to in the old drug store building?"

"Nothing helpful," Bert replied. "I've talked with the Rehsa brothers on a couple of occasions over the past few weeks and they tell me that they're making good progress on the apartments. Bob and Bud are working on the main floor conversion and the MIK guys are working on the upstairs renovation and the two new apartments in the basement. I had to be very careful not to let the brothers know we had any suspicions about the MIK guys, and I think I achieved that. And then, as you know Fred, we sent Bennie down to pay a visit one day. He was able to get in and chat with Bob and Bud and several of the MIK guys and everything seemed perfectly in order. I just don't know anything more we can do."

Fred replied, "Bert, maybe it would be good for you to go down there and snoop around. If you could come up with a good excuse to check-out the place it would sure make me feel better."

Bert thought for a minute, and said, "Well, I'll give it some thought and try and come up with a good reason. It couldn't hurt."

"And nothing new from the G-Men?" asked Fred.

"Nothing," replied the sheriff. "They've been out and about every day, but haven't learned anything new."

"Depressing," said Fred. He then smiled and added "But I've got a new one that'll cheer you up for the day!"

Kyle and Bert looked at him in anticipation.

Fred continued, "The story is about this elderly woman. She decided to prepare a will. She told her lawyer that she had two requests. Firstly, she wanted to be cremated, and secondly she wanted her ashes scattered about Wal-Mart. The lawyer scratched his head, said that was a bit strange, and asked her why. She told him that by doing that she would rest assured that her daughters would always visit her twice a week!"

Bert and Kyle laughed, stood, and Kyle said, "Sounds like a plan to me."

The two lawmen left Creech's for their office.

●●●

Same Day, 5 pm
Sheriff's Office
Harlan, Kentucky

Rosie Cain looked up at Preacher Puss and said, "Okay ole girl, it's time to head out for the weekend." She opened up the cat carrier and sat it on the floor. Preacher Puss quickly jumped down from her shelf and walked inside the carrier. Rosie closed the door on the carrier and said, "I do believe you really enjoy going home with me every weekend. And I just can't tell you how much I enjoy having you."

Preacher Puss meowed loudly. Rosie turned and said to Deputy Mousy Giles, "Hey Mousy, I'm off for the weekend. You and Bill hold down the fort." Mousy worked the office and Bill Black drove a cruiser on the second shift and on weekends.

Mousy replied, "Yeah, you girls have a good weekend."

Rosie, with cat carrier in hand, headed home. Her husband, a salesman who spend a lot of time traveling, would not be home this weekend and Rosie was looking forward to a nice, quiet couple of days with Preacher Puss.

• • •

Same Day, 8 pm
Old Drug Store Building
Harlan, Kentucky

The 10 North Koreans had gathered once again around their make-shift table on the first floor. They had just finished dinner and were going to hear an update from General Jung.

"I'm very pleased to be able to report that all our plans are going exactly as scheduled. I talked this morning with Supreme Leader Kim and he told me to thank each of you and to keep up the good work. He assured me we will each be greatly rewarded if our missions are completed successfully. Firstly, regarding our tunnel. We have now completed it to a point under the street and starting now toward the Memorial building. If all goes well we should be directly under the center of the building and up to the bottom of the concrete slab floor in about another 10 days. We'll then have to wait until Saturday evening, October 3, to drill the hole in the floor. It's been a very difficult tunnel to dig, and certainly is taking longer than would be normal if we had more equipment, but we are accomplishing it. The dirt that has been removed has been stacked up in our secret area behind the apartment's false back wall, and we have plenty of room remaining for the rest of the dirt. Fortunately, the sheriff or no one else has had reason to take a look at our operation in the basement. But if they do, I'm confident they won't discover what we're doing behind the false wall. Secondly, General Rhee assures me that the plan to take out the deserters is going well and will be executed on the night of Saturday, October 3. And lastly, General Yi has in place his plans for sheriff Sterling. Yi, why don't you share those with everyone."

"Thank you General Jung," Yi said. "Yes, were are ready to execute our primary plan this weekend. Hopefully, if it goes well we will no longer have Sheriff Sterling to contend with. The mission planned for this weekend involves the kidnapping, or catnapping if you prefer, of the Sheriff's mascot. Her name is Preacher Puss. We have learned that there is a deputy sheriff in the office named Deputy Cain who takes the cat home with her on weekends. We have learned where she lives, in a subdivision called Sunny Acres. She has a large back yard that she had fenced with special high fencing so she could put the cat out for exercise and not worry about her escaping over the fence. My assistant, Park, will enter her back yard and entice the cat into a carrier. Park will leave a ransom note in the back yard and then bring the cat to me. The ransom note will say if they want the cat back alive the sheriff will bring an envelope with $5,000 in it to a location we have selected. Park and I will meet the sheriff at the location on Sunday night at 10 pm. When the sheriff walks out to the drop-point with the envelope he will be shot. We have every reason to believe that this plan will work, but if for any reason it fails we do have a good back-up plan. I think we are all set."

Jung said, "Thank you General Yi. And thank each of you for your continued devoted effort to accomplish our mission. You are dismissed."

● ● ●

Saturday, September 19, 4 pm
Sunny Acres Subdivision
Harlan County, Kentucky

Park Ji-min looked very carefully all around. He had left his car a block away and had walked to Deputy Rosie Cain's home. He first walked casually down the street, and then when he was almost to Rosie's house he looked behind to check if anyone might be following. They were not. He quickly ducked in to the side of Rosie's house and toward the back. Fortunately, there were no windows on this side of her home. When he got to the fence door leading into the back yard he stopped and looked carefully through the crack to see if anyone was in the yard. No one but the cat was there. He sat the carrier down on the ground, opened its door, then lifted the latch locking the fence door and opened it just enough to slide the pet carrier inside. He then closed the fence door and watched through the crack. He saw Preacher Puss look at the carrier, and then walk over to it. She smelled it, and then after several seconds decided to walk inside it. Quickly, Park opened the fence door, reached down and closed the carrier door, and slid it back out the fence. He then closed and latched the fence door. He looked at the pet carrier and through the air holes could see the big gray cat inside. Preacher Puss meowed loudly. Park said, "Be quiet cat....you'll be okay." He grabbed the ransom note from his pocket and tossed it over the fence. He then picked up the carrier and headed for his car.

• • •

One hour later

Rosie was crying uncontrollably. Bert hugged her and said, "Rosie, it's not your fault. Don't you worry, we'll get her back. I promise."

The two were standing in Rosie's back yard. She had called him immediately after coming out and finding Preacher Puss missing. She saw the envelope on the ground. After reading it she placed the call. Bert had arrived in less than ten minutes.

Bert said, "Rosie, lets go inside and think about this. I assure you our cat will be safely returned." Rosie sobbed, and then nodded agreement. The two walked into her house. Bert got her a glass of water and the two sat on the sofa together.

Bert opened and again read the ransom note:

Dear Deputy Cain. We have your cat. If you want her back alive you must do as we say.

You must have Sheriff Sterling put $5,000 in one hundred dollar bills into an envelope and bring it to the parking lot of the closed store called Jim's Junk. He must park directly in front of the store, get out of his car and await our instructions. He must come alone. If anyone comes with him or if you fail to follow these instructions the cat will be killed.

He must arrive at Jim's Junk Store at exactly 10 pm tomorrow night.

Rosie continued to cry. Bert said, "Rosie, please believe me, she'll be okay. I'll get the money and we'll get ole Preacher Puss back tomorrow night. Once we have her back then we'll figure out who did it and how we can get them. I won't take any chances. They'll cooperate in order to get the money. Okay?"

Rosie looked at Bert through wet, red eyes and nodded.

• • •

Sunday, September 20, 9 pm
Sunny Acres Subdivision
Harlan County, Kentucky

Rosie, Carolyn Potter, Kyle Potter, and sheriff Sterling sat in Rosie's living room. Rosie looked at Carolyn and said, "We sure thank you Carolyn. It would likely have been impossible for us to put together $5,000 in cash in such a short time without your help."

Carolyn said, "I love Preacher Puss almost as much as I love Bert. I'm just glad I work at the bank and was able to get our President, Calvin Brown, to loan me $5,000 in one hundred dollar bills, and that he was willing to do it immediately and with no questions asked. Mr. Brown is the one to thank."

Bert replied, "Yeah, Calvin is a good egg. We owe him for his cooperation on this." He looked at the large envelope in his hand.

Kyle said, "That old Jim's Junk Store seems a funny place for them to want to have the exchange."

Bert replied, "I think they likely scouted it out pretty good. As you know, it's located remotely starting up Pine Mountain on highway 421. There are no other houses close, and the forest is all around it. And in addition to the entrance off 421 there is a gravel road from the back of the store that comes out in Baxter, about a mile's drive. I figured they might use that gravel road, and thought about maybe having someone block it, but it just seemed too dangerous. If something went wrong and Preacher Puss got killed I'd just never forgive myself. I still think the best course is to just go along with the kidnapper and worry about trying to capture him after we get our cat back."

Rosie patted Bert on the back and said, "Bert, thank you so much for your help. I know you love that cat as much as I do."

Bert replied, "Well, speaking of her, I think I'd best get headed to Jim's Junk Store. The note said for me to arrive at 10 pm sharp, and I don't want to keep em waiting."

Bert stood up with the cash filled envelope in his hand. He shook Kyle's hand, hugged Rosie, and hugged and kissed Carolyn. He said, "You guys just wait right here. Hopefully I'll be back shortly with our favorite cat. Prayers would be appreciated!"

Kyle and the two ladies nodded vigorously. Carolyn said, "You know those prayers will be going up until you return. Please be safe."

Bert turned, walked out to his car, and headed for Jim's Junk Store.

● ● ●

Same Day, 9:45 pm
Jim's Junk Store, Highway 421
Harlan County, Kentucky

Yi and Park had just arrived. Park was driving. He pulled their car to the right side of the old dilapidated building, and parked pointed toward the gravel road in the back. The two got out with Park carrying the pet carrier and Yi carrying a small folding chair. Yi walked about a dozen steps along the front of the store, unfolded the chair and sat it in the parking lot. He then returned beside their car and said to Park, "Let me tell you one last time what we're going to do. The sheriff will pull his car directly in front of the store. When he gets out I'll shout to him to bring the money and place it in the chair. If he does that, then I'll shoot him when he gets to the chair. More likely he'll want to see the cat first. If so I'll have to get her out of the carrier, otherwise the sheriff wouldn't be able to see her. We've already put a collar and leash on her, so I'll grab the leash and walk out far enough for him to see her. Then I'll walk back here beside the car. At that point you go ahead and get in the car under the wheel, ready for a fast get away. When he then walks to the chair with the money I'll shoot him and then jump in the car and we'll head down the back road. Is that clear?"

Park said, "Yes General Yi, very clear."

Yi looked at his watch. It indicated 9:57. It was very dark, but the full moon provided enough light to see. Very few cars were traveling at this hour on highway 421.

Suddenly a headlight appeared. The car then slowly pulled into the parking lot. Clearly it was the sheriff's cruiser. Bert saw a car and two men at the right side of the building. As he pulled directly into the center parking space he noticed a chair positioned about midway between his car and the men. He slowly got out of his car. He shut the car door and looked over the top of his cruiser toward the two men.

Yi then shouted, "Bring the money and put it in the chair."

Bert replied, "No way. You show me the cat!"

Yi held up the pet carrier.

Bert shouted, "Can't see the cat. Get her out."

Park then opened the carrier door, grabbed the leash and pulled Preacher Puss out. He handed the leash to Yi. Yi then walked a couple of steps toward the chair and said, "As you can see, sheriff, the cat's just fine. But she'll be dead shortly if you don't bring that money to the chair." He turned and walked back to the car, holding the leash in his left hand. He then turned to see what the sheriff was going to do.

Bert raised the money envelope in his hand and shouted, "Okay, I'm bringing the money to the chair. When I do, you bring the cat out here and we'll make the exchange."

"You do that," shouted Yi.

Bert started walking slowly toward the chair.

Park jumped in the car's driver seat.

Yi held the cat's leash tightly in his left hand and slowly moved his right hand to the pistol stuck in his belt. He removed the pistol and brought it up ready to fire.

With all the force she could muster Preacher Puss sprung from the ground and flew through the air directly toward Yi's hand. With claws on all four paws extended she landed perfectly on his wrist. All claws dug in deeply with several cutting into veins. Blood starting spewing everywhere. Yi screamed, dropped the gun, and then ran around the car and jumped in the passenger side. "Get the hell out of here," he said to Park.

Park already had the motor running. He stomped the accelerator and the car spun off down the gravel road toward Baxter.

Bert ran to the corner of the building and grabbed Preacher Puss's leash. The cat looked up at him with huge eyes and began swishing her tail and purring loudly. Bert said, "Ole girl, you've done it again. Let's get you home to Rosie."

● ● ●

Same Day, 10:45 pm
Sunny Acres Subdivision
Harlan, Kentucky

Kyle, Carolyn, and Rosie were quietly sitting in the living room. No one had said anything for some time. All eyes were downcast.

Suddenly the front door opened and Preacher Puss came bounding into the room. She headed straight for Rosie and jumped up into her lap. Rosie hugged her tightly, started crying, and whispered, "Thank you Lord!"

Bert walked to Rosie and said, "What about me?"

Still holding tightly to Preacher Puss with her left arm, Rosie stood and stretched her right arm around Bert in a big hug. She said, "After the Lord, you're second. Thank you. Thank you. Thank you."

Carolyn then gave Bert a big kiss and tight embrace. She said, "Are we ever so glad to see you two. Our prayers are answered!"

Kyle next hugged Bert and said, "Sheriff, we can't wait to hear your story. We know the happy ending, but we're all ears to hear how it came down."

The four then took seats. Preacher Puss moved from one to another allowing each to show their affection. Bert then gave them a blow by blow account of what had happened. When he finished, everyone looked at Preacher Puss.

Kyle said, "How absolutely amazing is that cat! I guess the bad guys hadn't been told about her aversion to guns!"

"Thank the good Lord for that," Rosie said, "Otherwise, ole Bert might not now be with us."

Bert replied, "Absolutely. Preacher Puss's instincts are beyond remarkable. You should have heard that bad guy yell when she hit him. And I'll bet they never get all the blood up in that parking lot, and also in the get-away car."

Everyone continued to gently stroke Preacher Puss. She purred her approval.

Carolyn then looked at Bert and asked, "I hope you didn't forget to pick up that envelope!"

Bert laughed and said, "I got it. It's in my car. Don't let me forget to give it to you on our way out. I'm sure Calvin Brown will be happy to see it tomorrow morning."

Kyle then said, "So it went just perfectly. Only thing is the bad guys got away. But at least one of them has some wounds. Maybe we can spot him."

Bert said, "Yeah, and I heard his voice too. But right now, I'm just pleased as punch to have ole Preacher Puss safely back home and no bullet holes in me. We'll worry about the bad guys a little later.

All nodded agreement.

Chapter 10

Monday, September 21, 9 am
Sheriff's Office
Harlan, Kentucky

Mayor Fred Knapp, Harlan Police Chief Big Boy Asher, Deputy Kyle Potter, and the two G-Men were seated in the sheriff's office. Bert had called the meeting early this morning. Rosie had just served coffee and returned to the reception area.

Bert looked at the five gentlemen, smiled, and said, "Guys, I appreciate so much your speedy convening this morning. I wanted to give you an update on yesterday's events, and then get your take on what we should do."

He continued, "Kyle knows what I'm about to relate to you, but I wanted him here for his input." Bert then told the group all the details about yesterday's attempted catnapping and the attempt on his life.

The men listened intently. Chief Asher then said, "So it's pretty clear that stealing the cat was just bait to lure you to that remote area and kill you. And it sounded to me like they darn well just about did it. Preacher Puss to the rescue again! I can't wait to tell my guys about this one!"

Mayor Knapp said, "I think Big Boy summed it up pretty well. We've obviously got a big problem. Someone's out to kill our sheriff. And we think we know who it is, but we just can't prove any of it."

Cody Short said, "I have one thing to report that might help. When we heard about the company called MIK Properties we asked our guys to check them out. Sammy and I got a text message last night saying that the company does in fact exist, and is about 8 years old, but that the owner, Sammie Wong, is a close personal friend to Kim Jong-un."

All thought about this for a moment, and then Chief Asher said, "The sheriff has briefed me on everything about this MIK group working in the old drug store building. With this new information that the owner is a close friend to Kim do you think we could arrest them?"

Bert replied, "I just don't know. We've sure got a lot of circumstantial evidence, but I have no idea if it would be enough to shut em down." He looked at Kyle and said, "Kyle, what's your opinion?"

The chief deputy replied, "I think it's a fine line. My suggestion would be to present what we know to Judge Oakes and get his opinion. And then we go from there."

All the group nodded approval. Bert said, "That sounds good to me. I think I'll head right over to his chambers when we conclude. Does anyone have anything else?"

Sammy King said, "Two weeks from right now the festival will be all over. I still feel like the bad guys have additional plans, and I'm really concerned. Regardless of what Judge Oakes may say, I feel that those 10 MIK guys are at the bottom of all our problems. It would be great if the Judge gives the green light to arrest them, but if he doesn't I think we've really got to keep them closely under surveillance."

Bert said, "Good thought Sammy. Anyone else?"

All were quiet. Bert stood and said, "Thanks again for being here. I'm headed to see the Judge, and I'll keep you posted."

Preacher Puss was resting comfortably in her bed on the shelf near the entrance door. As each of the group departed they reached up and gently stroked the cat. She purred her approval.

● ● ●

Same Day, 10 am
Judge Oakes' Chambers
Harlan, Kentucky

Fortunately, the Judge did not have anything on his docket until afternoon. Sheriff Sterling was ushered into his chambers by his clerk.

"Well, well, well. I do believe it's the sheriff of Harlan County," Judge Oakes proclaimed.

"Have a seat Bert and I'll get us some coffee."

The judge walked over to a corner in his chambers where there was a table with coffee service on it. He got out two cups and poured them full. He asked, "Cream or sugar?"

"No, black'll be fine Judge."

After the coffee was served the judge asked, "So what brings you here this fine morning?"

Bert relayed all the information he knew about the MIK Properties company and their operation at the old drug store. He then told the judge about the incident last night.

Judge Oakes got a very sour look on his face and said, "Bert, they tried to kill you!"

"They did. And they came close. But thanks to our miracle cat I survived."

The judge chuckled and said, "You better keep that cat satisfied and on the job!"

"You got that right," replied Bert. "My big question to you is do we have enough to shut those guys down?

Judge Oakes thought for a minute, squirmed in his chair, and said "As much as it pains me to say this, no, you do not have sufficient evidence to arrest or shut them down. The fact that the owner of the company is a good friend with Kim Jong-un certainly is troubling, but is not actionable. And from what you've conveyed to me none of the 10 guys have actually been caught breaking any laws. We could likely prove their papers are illegal, but they'd be out on bail within an hour and that certainly wouldn't help us any. I know they smell really rotten, and very likely are, but as things stand right now our laws would not support any action against them that would keep them in jail till after the festival. I'm sorry to have to tell you this."

Bert nodded and said, "I understand. It's what I thought you'd say. And I agree. But it sure is frustrating. I guess we'll just have to keep trying to find something concrete. And we've only got a short time before the festival."

The judge said, "So you think their being here is somehow tied to the festival?"

"The information we have received, and it comes from the CIA Director and another excellent source, is that they likely are planning something related to it."

Judge Oakes stood, extended his hand to Bert and said, "Sheriff, I've got every confidence in you and your operation. I wish you the best of luck."

The two men shook hands Bert thanked the judge and headed back to his office.

•••

Thursday, September 24
Center for Appalachian Research
Lexington, Kentucky

CIA Director Snell had just been ushered into Dr. Randy Peters' office. Director Snell carried a brief case. He walked over to a table beside Dr. Peters' desk and placed the brief case on it. He opened it and said, "Behold the fake anchor crosses!"

Randy's eyes got large as he reached to pick up one of the beautiful, golden crosses. He said, "My, my, my. If I didn't know all six of mine are here in my Center I'd think you stole them! These are magnificent." He then replaced the one, and grabbed another. He held it up and examined it closely. It was the duplicate of the Helena Anchor Cross. This was the one that looked exactly like the other five except on one side the original had wood added that had been from the cross on which Christ was crucified and expertly carved to attach and fit perfectly on one side of the golden anchor cross. The duplicate that Randy was now examining looked identical to the original. He kept closely looking at every detail and rotating the artifact around in his hand.

Finally he said, "Max, your craftsmen have accomplished what I thought would be impossible to do. They have made six anchor crosses absolutely identical in every respect to the six originals that I possess. Congratulations!"

Max beamed and said, "That's the best news I could hear. If you can't tell them from the originals then I'm certain no one else will be able to. With your permission I believe we can safely substitute these at this year's ACFesV."

"After examining them, I think they will work perfectly. One week from tomorrow I will lock all the originals up in my safe and take these duplicates on my trip to Harlan and get them set up in the Seibert Memorial. Those viewing them will never know the difference, and we'll have eliminated the chance for the bad guys to steal the originals."

Max said, "Thanks so much Dr. Peters. I really appreciate your cooperation. You and I will be the only two people that will know the anchor crosses at ACFes V are duplicates."

•••

Friday, September 25
Harlan, Kentucky

Bert was walking down Central Street toward the old drug store building. He was dreading the confrontation with the MIK Properties people, but he felt he had to take some action and decided to just go for a visit and see what he might discover. He looked at his watch and saw it was about 10 am. Everyone there should be at work.

He knocked on the entrance door.

It opened and Bud Rehsa smiled at him and said, "Bert, good to see you. I hope it's another social visit."

Bert grinned, shook hands with Bud, and said, "Sure is. I hadn't stopped by for a while and just was curious to see what progress you boys were making."

They walked into the building. Bob Rehsa walked over, shook hands, and said, "Bert, we're just ready for a good break. Your timing is perfect. Let me show you around here."

Bob and Bud took the sheriff on a tour of the four apartments they had been working on. After the tour they pulled up chairs and seated themselves. Bert said, "Guys, you do really good work. These apartments look very, very nice. It looks like about all you've got left to do are the finishing touches."

"True," Bob said. "But those finishing touches can take a lot of work. They're what makes the real difference between a shoddy job and a really nice one."

Bert thought a moment and said, "How are the MIK guys doing on the other apartments?"

"Really don't know for sure," Bud said. "They've been working mighty hard, but frankly we don't have much interaction. They stay upstairs or in the basement most all the time. We rarely see them."

"Think I could take a look there?" asked the sheriff.

Bob said, "I'm sure that would be fine. Just go over and knock on that basement door and one of the guys will come up and show you down."

"Thanks," Bert replied as he stood and started walking toward the basement door. "It was good talking to you. I'll let you get back to work."

Bert first tried the knob on the door, but when he found it to be locked he knocked loudly. It was a couple of minutes before anyone came to open it. General Rhee looked stunned when he saw the sheriff standing there. He said, "Mr. Sheriff, is there a problem?"

Bert said, "Not that I know of. I was just paying a social visit. Just curious about the progress you guys were making. Bob and Bud showed me around the first floor. It looks just super. I was hoping I might see the basement and the upstairs."

Rhee thought a few seconds and said, "Certainly. Some of our guys are out running errands, but I'll be glad to show you. Please follow me down."

"Thanks," Bert replied as the two of them walked down the stairs.

Rhee said, "As you can see, we've made progress down here, but less than the Rehsas. Those boys are really professional. We're much slower."

The Sheriff looked around and saw all the walls up for the two apartments. He walked through first the East unit and then went to the West apartment. He said, "Yeah, you guys are a bit behind Bob and Bud, but at least things seem to be coming along." It was then that he noticed the service door in the back wall of the bedroom. He asked, "That's a funny place for a door!"

Perspiration had formed on Rhee's forehead. He answered, "That's just a service door to the utility closet. Plumbing, electrical panels, and stuff."

"I see," Bert replied as he walked over to the door. He grabbed the door knob and tried to open it. But it was locked."

Rhee was both sweating and looking a bit pale. He said, "I guess Jung locked it. I don't have a key....sorry."

"No problem," Bert said. "Just curious."

He turned and started walking out, followed closely by Rhee.

They walked back up to the main floor, and then upstairs to the four apartments. When Bert got up he tried to walk into the first apartment, but it too was locked.

Rhee said, "Oh, sorry. These are currently being used as our sleeping quarters, and we keep them locked. I do have a key to the one I'm in over there," he said as he pointed to the adjacent apartment. The two walked there, Rhee opened the door, and they walked in.

Bert took a look around and said, "I don't remember exactly what these upstairs units looked like before. I was just here for a very short tour, but I can't tell much progress in this unit."

Rhee replied, "No, we haven't started on this unit yet. We're working in another one presently. The unit here that I'm in is scheduled for last."

"I understand," the sheriff replied. "Are you the only MIK person here right now?"

"Yes, as I told you, the others have gone on errands to get supplies."

"Interesting," Bert replied, as he turned and started toward the steps going back down to the main floor. Rhee shut his door and locked it and followed the sheriff down the stairs.

When they were on the main floor standing by the door Bert shouted to the Rehsa brothers, "You guys work hard....I'll see you later." They shouted their good-byes.

He then shook hands with Rhee and said, "I do appreciate your taking the time to tour me around. The apartments are going to be very nice. I'm sure I'll be able to recommend them to some of my friends."

Rhee replied, "Thank you Mr. Sheriff. It was a pleasure."

Bert turned and walked out, headed back to his office.

● ● ●

Same Day, 8 pm
Old Drug Store Building
Harlan, Kentucky

After learning of the sheriff's visit General Rhee was being drilled by General Jung. "Rhee, are you sure the sheriff didn't see anything he thought suspicious? We are only about a week away now from achieving our mission... we sure don't need trouble."

All ten North Koreans were gathered again for a meeting after having had dinner.

Rhee replied, "He wanted to see both the basement and the upstairs. The brothers had already shown him the main floor, and he seemed to think their progress was excellent. I first took him to the basement. He seemed satisfied, although he noted our progress was a bit slow. He then saw our secret door and asked what it was. I told him it was a service door to the utilities. He walked over and tried to open it. It's certainly a good thing we keep it locked at all times. I told him I did not have a key. I was really worried that you guys working back there might make noise that he could hear. Fortunately, all was quiet. He seemed satisfied, and we then went upstairs. I told him I only had a key to my apartment and we looked in there. He said he saw no progress toward renovation. I told him we were working on the other apartments and that mine would be the last to be renovated. He appeared satisfied with that, and then he left."

"I sure wish Yi had finished him off last Sunday," Jung said. "I think he's very suspicious of our work. Fortunately, he heard no noise from our drilling operations.

That could have been very bad. At least we survived his visit. I will report that to our Supreme Leader tomorrow morning when I call him. Kim likely will not be pleased. And he's still steaming over the failed attempt to take out the sheriff last Sunday." Jung looked sternly at General Yi.

General Yi looked at his heavily bandaged wrist. It was still throbbing. That cat had certainly done her damage. He then said, "The sheriff will not survive our plan for him next weekend. He is a dead man walking."

General Jung laughed and said, "Yi, you've been watching too many Hollywood movies. But I sure hope you know what's at stake on your next attempt. As you are well aware, the Supreme Leader does not tolerate failure."

Yi nodded. Jung continued, "So, other than those things, I think all else is on schedule. Today we arrived with the tunnel at the coordinates directly below the center of the Memorial Building. Starting tomorrow we'll start vertically digging until we reach the bottom of the concrete slab floor. That shouldn't take more than two or three days. So we'll be well ahead of schedule and then have to just wait until next Saturday night to drill through the floor and get the golden artifacts. General Rhee assures me his plan for eliminating the deserters is all finalized and ready for execution next Saturday night. So everyone just continue to do your jobs and we'll be back home in just a little over a week. You are dismissed."

Chapter 11

Monday, September 28, 9 am

Creech Cafe

Harlan, Kentucky

Fred swatted at Polly. The bird had attempted to grab a bite of Kyle's donut. "You get back to your perch and stay there," he shouted.

"Bad bird, bad bird," Polly replied as she flew back to her perch.

Kyle grinned and said, "Polly just loves your donuts, Fred."

"Yeah, maybe I should take her mooching as a compliment!"

Bennie walked up with the coffee pot and started filling their cups, "You guys look a bit gloomy. Here's a joke to cheer you up. Did you know when you get a bladder infection urine trouble, that's U R I N E?"

Fred and the two lawmen looked up at Bennie. Bert said, "Bennie, you been out visiting Fatso lately? You better keep working on those jokes....I'm afraid you've got a ways to go to catch up with Fred."

Fred smiled, patted Bennie on the back and said, "You just keep working on it Bennie. It takes a while."

"So ACFesV starts this Friday," Fred said. "Everything with all the planning looks good, and even the weather is predicted to be super for this weekend. I've asked Pastor Bell to put in a special request to the good Lord for us."

Bert said, "We could well need it. We've still got those 10 MIK guys on the loose and we don't have an idea what they've got cooking."

The mayor asked, "You went to visit them last Friday. Did you see or hear anything at all that might help us?"

"I wish I could say yes, but honestly, they seem to have everything pretty well covered. When I got there I chatted a bit with Bud and Bob, but they didn't say that anything seemed out of place. And their four apartments on the first floor are really shaping up nicely. I asked about the ones in the basement and upstairs and they said I'd need to talk to one of the MIK guys. They told me to knock on the basement door. I did, and the same fellow opened the door that picked up the carry-out order when Carolyn and I were having dinner at The China Pan. I think his name is Rhee. He told me the others were running errands and he showed me the basement and upstairs. Everything looked okay. The progress in the basement looked a little slow, and they hadn't started on the one upstairs apartment that I saw. Rhee said they were working on the others and that his would be the last. All that seemed believable. But a couple of things didn't exactly add up. First, as I was entering the building I noticed that both their vehicles were parked in the loading zone. So I wondered how the guys traveled to where ever they were going on their errands. And secondly, as I left I walked by their car and looked in on the passenger side. I saw a lot of dark stains on and around the right arm rest. Sure looked like it could have been blood."

Kyle said, "Circumstantial. Everything still circumstantial. Nothing that we could charge them with."

Bert nodded and said, "True. And that's what is so frustrating. I wish I could have seen the license plate on that car at Jim's Junk Store, but it was just too dark. I couldn't even tell the make or color of the car. But I'd sure be willing to bet that the stains on the passenger side are blood from the guy that tried to shoot me. I'm sure if confronted they would just say the stains were the result of some kind of accident. Nothing we could dispute..... frustrating!"

"So where do you figure the other 9 guys were?" asked Fred.

"Now that is a very good question, Mr. Mayor. There was not hide nor hair of them anywhere in the building. It is possible, I suppose, that some could have been sleeping in their upstairs apartments, but surely not all 9. And I don't have any idea where they could have gone on foot here in town to get supplies. That's certainly a puzzler."

Fred said, "And nothing else on your tour of the building seemed out of place or unusual?"

Bert thought for a moment and then said, "There was this strange door that was in the back wall of the West apartment in the basement. I asked Rhee what it was and he said it was a door to the utility closet, but it was locked, and he said he didn't have a key."

Kyle said, "What would be strange about that?"

"Don't know, really," the sheriff replied. "Probably nothing, but there just seemed something a little off. Also, I noticed that Rhee was perspiring and his face color seemed a little pale while we were around that door."

The three were quiet for a couple of minutes. Bert then said, "We have no probable cause to go back over there and demand for the door to be opened. Judge Oakes certainly would not issue a search warrant based on the information I've just shared with you. So I guess we just keep on keeping on."

"I guess," Fred replied, "but I certainly don't have a real good feeling about those guys."

"One thing came to mind when Bennie's joke brought Fatso Chapel's name up a few minutes ago. When all else fails sometimes a visit with Trigger Green can shed some light on things. I think I just might make a trip to Maggard's Grocery."

Kyle and Fred nodded. Kyle said, "Wouldn't hurt.... except you'd have to listen to some of Fatso's jokes."

"I'm going to do it," Bert replied. "And speaking of jokes, I'm sure ole Fred here could easily top the one Bennie told us."

Fred smiled, nodded, and began, "This elderly couple was lying in bed one night. The lady felt romantic, but the husband was sound asleep. She punched him awake and said that he used to hold her hand. He reached across and held her hand briefly and then again started snoring. She punched him again and said he used to kiss her. He gave her a peck and then went back to sleep. She punched him a third time and reminded him how he used to bite her neck. He angrily threw back the covers and got out of bed.

Surprised, she asked where he was going. He said he was going to get his teeth."

The two lawmen laughed and stood. Bert said, "Thanks Fred. That'll hold us until we get to Maggard's and hear one from Fatso."

•••

Same Day, 10:30 am
Maggard's Grocery
Near Wallins, Kentucky

Fatso punched the intercom button and said to Trigger, "Bert Sterling and Kyle Potter just pulled into the parking lot."

Trigger replied, "Just send em back. I have no idea why they're here."

"Welcome, welcome, welcome," shouted Fatso as the two lawmen entered the store. "Trigger said for you to go on back. But first you gotta tell me why elephants don't like playing cards in the jungle?"

Both men grinned and shrugged their shoulders.

"Because of all the cheetahs," shouted Fatso with a chuckle.

Bert knocked on the door and pushed it open after Fatso released the lock. Trigger pushed back from his desk, stood, and walked around to shake hands. He said, "Good to see you both....please have a seat and we'll talk about anything you wish. Care for anything to drink?"

As the three took their seats Bert said, "No thanks Trigger, we just left Creech's. We're all saturated with Fred's coffee."

"Haven't seen you two for a while now. I hope I haven't slipped up and got caught doing something bad," Trigger said with a smile.

Kyle and Bert both grinned. Bert said, "No, not that I know of. I wanted to chat with you about something that could potentially cause a problem at the festival this year.... possibly even harm or kill some of our citizens."

Trigger got a very solemn look and said, "Let's hear it."

"It's in respect to the old drug store building at the corner of 1st and Central Streets. A company called MIK Properties bought the building and claims they are converting it to 10 apartment units. Are you aware of this?"

Trigger hesitated a moment and said, "Yes, I am. I was contracted to assist them. My understanding is that they are a foreign company, Chinese I believe, and needed help in buying the building. Fatso and I sort of acted as a real estate agent for them. We bought the building and then got the upstairs units livable....had a cleaning crew come in and spruce em up. And we got all the utilities going. Stuff like that. Sure didn't see anything wrong or illegal with doing that."

Bert asked, "And did you contact the Rehsa brothers to work there?"

"Yeah. They said they needed a couple of guys to help. I thought Bob and Bud would be perfect for them," replied Trigger.

"I see," said the sheriff. "And did you notice how much these guys look like the North Koreans that the Slusher brothers employ? The ones that were sent here by Kim Jong-un on various missions?"

Trigger started to feel uneasy about the visit. He said, "Of course. It'd be hard to miss. But I was told they were Chinese."

"They could be," Bert responded. "But they also could be North Koreans. And my office has reason to believe that they are here on some kind of mission associated with the festival. I just thought you might be able to shed a little light on things. I'm not accusing you of being involved with them. From what you've shared with me so far you would be in the clear, no more involved than

Bob and Bud. All I'm trying to do is prevent trouble and possibly harm or bloodshed."

Kyle looked at Bert and said, "Boss, why don't you also tell him what happened on Sunday before last."

Bert nodded, and then told Trigger about the catnapping and the attempt made on his life.

Trigger chuckled and said, "If ole Preacher Puss ever gets tired of working for you please just bring her over here. I'd love to have her." He then turned serious and continued, "Bert, I may well have stepped in it again. I really don't know. What I've told you is all I know. I have no knowledge about anything that group might be planning. I was simply employed to play realtor in getting that building for them. You know I won't reveal who hired me, but I can certainly tell you it wasn't the North Korean government."

Bert said, "I believe you, Trigger. I appreciate what you've told me. Please do keep your eyes and ears open. Knowing our suspicions, please give me a call if you learn anything that might help us."

"Bert, we've been friends for many years. You know I wouldn't knowingly be involved in anything that would do harm to anyone. I'll certainly let you know if I hear anything. I appreciate you guys dropping by."

All three stood, shook hands, and the lawmen left Trigger's office headed through the grocery store toward their car.

Fatso yelled, "Hey sheriff, you know why elephants are wrinkled?"

Bert replied, "Cause they're old?"

Fatso replied with a chuckle, "No, no. Cause they're too hard to iron. You boys take care."

Bert and Kyle shook their heads and left the store.

• • •

Same Time
Pyongyang, North Korea

The Supreme Leader had just finished dinner. He had polished off three quarter pounders, three large orders of fries, two chocolate milk shakes, and a chocolate sundae. He had given up watching what he ate.

He was alone in his office. After a huge burp, he reflected on where things stood with Project Gold Rush.

Other than the bungled attempt to kill sheriff Sterling, everything was going exactly as planned. This Saturday night everything would come together and his 10 soldiers would get those golden anchor crosses and kill the 10 deserters and the sheriff. They should then be back here by Wednesday night, October 7th. On Saturday, October 10th we will have the largest celebration in the history of North Korea. I will order hundreds of thousands of our citizens to attend the ceremony in the large parade area in front of my palace. There I will unveil the 6 golden anchor crosses. It will be a demonstration that will go down in history. It will the beginning of my world reign.

Kim dozed off to sleep in his chair....with a smile on his face.

• • •

Wednesday, September 30, 8 pm
Old Drug Store Building
Harlan, Kentucky

General Jung and the other 9 soldiers had finished work, taken showers, had dinner, and then gathered again for a meeting. Jung had a huge grin on his face. He was beaming as he said, "We did it!! The tunnel has now been completed to the bottom of the Memorial Building floor. We did run into some problems as we dug the vertical tunnel....hitting a lot of rock that caused problems, but we still managed to get finished 3 days before we drill through the floor. I want to congratulate my team. Excellent job!"

Everyone clapped loudly. Jung continued, "So now we can get some rest before finishing our missions on Saturday night. You may even wish to attend the festival. But for my report to Supreme Leader Kim in the morning, I would like for Generals Rhee and Yi to give me an update."

General Rhee said, "General Jung, we have our plans all complete. We will leave in the car on Saturday at 10:30 pm. We will drive to the Slusher Farm. Before we get to the guard gate I'll let Choe Chae-yeong out of the car to walk to the gate. I'll drive ahead, and when I get to the gate at approximately 11 pm I will encounter their guard. His name is George. He will open the window in his guard station and ask my business. I will say I'm lost and will ask for directions. While George gives me directions Choe will slip into the guard gate building and knock George unconscious. We did not want to shoot him because of the noise. Choe will tie and gag him. We will then open the gate and proceed to the large farm house. We know that everyone there normally goes to bed at 10 pm. It will be about 11:15 by the time we get there. Everyone should be asleep. We'll unload the explosive bomb and carry it behind the house where we'll place it in the gardening shed that is attached to the home. The timer will then be set to detonate at 1 pm. We should arrive back here around midnight."

"Excellent," Jung replied. He then looked to General Yi.

Yi said, "Our plan will begin to be executed on Saturday at just after midnight when the second shift at the sheriff's office goes off duty. Park and I will go to the back door at 12:15 am. Park will open the door. We have examined the lock previously and know that it is a simple passage lock, not a deadbolt. We have practiced opening it before and know it will not be a problem. After we enter, we will walk to the sheriff's office and rig our explosive bomb to the door between his office and the reception area. That door opens outward from the sheriff's office into the reception room. When we get everything set there will be a trip-wire attached from the bomb to the closed door. Opening the door will then trigger the bomb. Park and I should be back here by 12:30."

"What if someone opens the door on Sunday?" asked Jung.

"Our understanding is that the sheriff's office will be closed on Sunday for the festival. The sheriff and all his deputies will be working security. The next person to open the door to the sheriff's office should be Bert Sterling on Monday morning. He will then be history," replied Yi.

Jung rubbed his hands together and said, "Excellent, excellent. You have all done well. I will report our status tomorrow morning to the Supreme Leader. I'm sure he will be pleased and a great reward will await us in Pyongyang. You are dismissed."

Chapter 12

Thursday, October 1, 2 am
Harlan, Kentucky

Trigger was all alone in his car. He was approaching the Harlan bypass. He was deep in thought. After the visit from Bert and Kyle last Monday he had been very troubled that perhaps the 10 guys he and Fatso assisted might be planning something that could injure or kill people, and perhaps even many of his friends. He didn't want that to happen. When he went to bed last night he couldn't sleep. He finally decided he just had to find out what those guys were up to. He got dressed and drove to the grocery. He went in, walked back to his office, and from the key cabinet he removed one of the two extra keys

Fatso had made to the old drug store building. He left the store and proceeded toward Harlan.

He turned off the by-pass onto Mound Street, then to 1st Street where he turned right. Just before reaching the post office he turned right into their driveway that circled the building. He drove around back and parked in an empty space. He grabbed his flashlight and got out of the car. It was very dark and quiet. Nothing stirring at this hour of the morning. He quietly closed the car door and started walking toward 1st Street where he then turned right down the sidewalk beside the Indiana tagged car and van to the corner of the block. He was now at the entrance to the old drug store. He turned on his flashlight and slid the key into the lock. He slowly turned the key and then tried turning the door knob. It opened. He kept the flashlight pointed down and entered the store, closing the door behind him. He walked through one of the unfinished apartments and came to a space where steps going up appeared off to his right, and a door off to the left that he guessed went down to the basement. He walked over to the door, reached down and tried to turn the knob. He felt an excruciating pain from his head. His world then went dark. He could feel himself falling....and then nothing.

Jung dropped the baseball bat and said, "Turn the damn lights on. I want to see this visitor."

Park walked over to the wall switch and turned on the lights.

Jung, Park, and Yi all looked down at Trigger as he lay flat on the floor. Jung said, "That's the guy from the grocery store, Mr. Green! Wonder why he was snooping around here?"

General Yi said, "I have no idea, but I do know he'll be mad as hell when he wakes up. What're we gonna do with him?"

"Our mission is nearing completion. We can't take any chances now that would bring the law here. Let's tie and gag him and then take him down behind the false wall. We'll just leave him there. Once we're gone they'll find him. He'll be okay for three days."

The three carried Trigger down the stairs to the basement and into the West apartment to the back wall. Jung then unlocked the door and they carried him behind the false wall to the end of the stack of dirt and dumped him on the floor.

Jung said, "He'll be sore and uncomfortable, but that serves him right for breaking into our property. I'd have shot him, but the noise would have brought the police. We sure don't need that. We'll just leave him here."

Park and Yi nodded. The three left the secret work area, locked the door, and went back upstairs to bed.

•••

Same Day, 8 am
Maggard's Grocery
Near Wallins, Kentucky

Fatso had just opened the store. He had noticed that Trigger's car wasn't parked in the lot, but that wasn't unusual...he often didn't come in until a little later. After sweeping the store he got all comfortable in his chair at the check-out counter when he heard the door bell jingle, indicating someone had entered the store. He looked over and saw it was Mrs. Cavanaugh again.

"Hey Mrs. Cavanaugh, how you doing this morning?"

"Fine, thank you, Fatso," she replied. "I needed to bake a cake and was out of the mix I wanted. Just take me a second."

"No rush," he replied.

A few minutes later Mrs. Cavanaugh walked to the check-out counter with a box of cake mix in one hand and a can of soup in the other. As she placed the two items on the counter she said, "I thought I'd try this soup too.".

Fatso replied, "Sure. That reminds me of a good one, Mrs. Cavanaugh. Do you know what's red and white on the outside and gray and white on the inside?"

Mrs. Cavanaugh smiled and said, "I really don't, Fatso.

"Campbell's Cream of Elephant soup," he said with a chuckle.

"Oh Fatso, that sounds terrible. I'll try to not think about it when I eat this soup."

"That comes to four dollars, Mrs. Cavanaugh."

She paid him. "Thank you Mrs. Cavanaugh, you have a great day!"

She left the store. Fatso resumed his comfortable position in the chair. He was soon sound asleep. When he awoke it was almost 10 am. He looked again in the parking lot and didn't see Trigger's car. He pulled out his cell phone and gave him a call. No answer. He thought that very unusual, Trigger most always immediately answered a call from him. He thought for a moment trying to remember if Trigger had told him anything he was going to be doing this morning, but nothing came to mind. He thought, *if I don't hear from him by noon I'll have to start checking on him.*

● ● ●

Same Day, 9 am
Sheriff's Office
Harlan, Kentucky

Bert, Kyle, and Fred were in the sheriff's office. Rosie had served them coffee. Bert said, "Fred, I know you're busier than a one-armed paper hanger today, with the opening of the festival tomorrow and all, but I had a call earlier this morning from our friend Joe Chang and wanted to run it by the two of you to get your take. Joe told me his sources informed him that Kim Jong-un was now planning a huge celebration in front of his palace in Pyongyang on Saturday, October 10th. Joe couldn't find out the exact purpose of the gathering, but did learn that Kim said it would involve a world shaking announcement and demonstration. It's the timing that bothers me. That would be less than a week after our festival. Too big a coincidence to ignore. Any thoughts?"

Fred and Kyle looked puzzled. Fred said, "I bet it has to do with the golden anchor crosses. If those MIK guys stole them at the festival they would have just about enough time to get back to North Korea and have them displayed on October 10th."

Kyle nodded. Bert smiled and said, "That's exactly my take too, Fred. But I just don't see any way they could successfully steal them. We've got really good security guarding the Seibert Memorial. And even when it's closed we have guards stationed outside. I really don't know anything more we can do.....do you?"

Kyle and Fred thought. Fred said, "Can't think of anything else. What about you Kyle?"

"Yeah, I think we're in good shape. In addition to the guards that will be stationed at the Memorial, we've got all kinds of other security close enough that if anything developed they could come running and be there in just a couple of minutes," Kyle said.

The sheriff said, "Well, I'm sorry to bother you this morning Fred. But I thought this important enough to justify a brief meeting. Is everything else on track for the festival opening tomorrow?"

"It is," the mayor replied. "ACFesV kicks off at 1 pm tomorrow afternoon and goes until 3 pm on Sunday. Dr. Peters is scheduled to arrive in the morning with the six anchor crosses. He'll be bringing them via State Police helicopter. They'll land on the helipad on the court house roof and be escorted by several troopers to the memorial to get them all set up. The 30 national guard and state police sent by Governor Atherton will be reporting in around 9 am here to your office for assignments Bert. I think everything looks good."

Kyle added, "I understand we're expecting a really good turnout this year. From what I hear you can't get a motel room anywhere in Eastern Kentucky. I was talking yesterday with Chief Asher and he said they were anticipating big time traffic, but he seemed to think they could handle it just fine."

The mayor said, "So far, so good. But I think I'm getting a little old to be doing this. Next year I may hand it over to someone a little younger."

Bert laughed and said, "That'll never happen, Fred. Nobody could do it like you."

"Well, I thank you for your confidence anyway," the mayor said. "But speaking of getting old reminds me of one I heard yesterday. A lady had just turned 105 years old and was being interviewed by reporters. One asked her what was the best thing about being 105 years old. She said no peer pressure!"

The three laughed, stood and walked together into the reception area, headed toward the entrance door. Fred reached up and gave Preacher Puss a pet. She meowed loudly and swished her tail. Rosie yelled, "Mr. Mayor, you're one of her favorite people!"

"Thanks Rosie, you all take care," Fred said as he walked out the door.

•••

Same Day, 2 pm
Maggard's Grocery
Near Wallins, Kentucky

Fatso was becoming agitated. He had tried calling Trigger three more times without any answer. He had left a message each time for Trigger to call him back immediately. Something wasn't right....he could feel it. Trigger just didn't disappear like this. It had never happened before. Fatso decided he'd call his buddy Austin David to ask if he'd come and mind the store while he went into town to try and locate Trigger.

He walked back to Trigger's office to pick up the key to the store's pickup truck. Fatso figured he might as well burn the store's gas rather than his own. He was, after all, on store time. When he got to the key cabinet about to grab the truck keys he happened to notice that one of the keys to the old drug store was missing. He knew Trigger kept two of them. He grabbed the other one along with the truck keys and walked back to the check-out counter. He pulled out his cell phone and called Austin David.

• • •

Same Day, 30 minutes later
Sheriff's Office
Harlan, Kentucky

Rosie looked when she heard the door open. "Fatso! What are you doing here in the middle of the day. Is Trigger minding the store?"

Fatso reached up, gave Preacher Puss a nice, gentle stroke and said, "No, that's the problem Rosie. Trigger's missing! Can I talk with Bert?"

Preacher Puss purred loudly.

"Sure Fatso, go right on in. He's available."

Fatso walked to the office door and knocked. Bert said, "Please come in."

"Fatso, what a pleasure. Have a seat. Can I get you anything to drink?" the sheriff asked.

"No thanks Bert. I've got a problem. Trigger's missing." He continued then to relate to the sheriff the details. He did not, however, tell him about the two keys to the old drug store.

"I thought he might have dropped by to see you, or maybe called or something," Fatso said.

Bert frowned and said, "No, Fatso, I'm sorry to say I haven't heard a word from him. But I'll sure keep my ears open and let you know if I hear anything."

"Appreciate it, Bert," he replied. "It's just not like him to take off like this and not let me know. I feel something bad has happened."

"I'll tell Rosie to ask all the deputies to keep an eye out for him. Someone will see him. You just hang in there."

Fatso stood, shook hands with Bert, and said, "Okay. You let me know as soon as you learn anything."

"Sure will," Bert replied. Fatso turned and walked out headed back to the store.

● ● ●

Driving back to Maggard's Grocery Fatso thought, *If I don't hear something from Trigger or Bert by midnight I'm going to take this key and go slip into that old drug store building and see if they might have Trigger. Maybe I should have mentioned the keys to the sheriff, but I didn't want to cause Trigger any trouble. I'll just handle it myself. I sure hope Trigger's okay.*

• • •

Same Day, 11:45 pm
Near Wallins, Kentucky

Fatso had been at home since closing the store. He had been sitting in his lazy-boy hoping that Trigger would call. He did not. He reached down, grabbed his shoes, and put them on. He had the key. He headed for his car.

Twenty minutes later he pulled into the post office driveway and around to the back. And then he saw it...... there was Trigger's car! He thought, *I knew it. I just knew those MIK guys got him.* After parking his car he reached under his seat and got the gun. He slipped it under his belt. He grabbed a flashlight from the glove compartment, opened the car door, and started walking toward the old drug store building.

After getting to the entrance door he got out the key and put it in the lock. When he turned the key and tried the door knob it opened. He slowly entered the store, keeping his flashlight pointed down. He walked through one of the unfinished apartments and then stopped after getting to an open area where stairs going up were to his right and a door, presumably to the basement, was on his left. He knew the 10 guys would be up the stairs in their apartments, and hopefully asleep. He thought he'd check out the basement first. He tried the door knob, but it was locked. He then felt a stabbing pain as someone busted him on the head. All went dark as he fell to the floor.

Jung dropped the baseball bat and said, "Got another one! Turn on the light."

General Yi flipped the light switch on the wall.

"It's that strange one from the grocery store," Jung said.

Yi asked, "What'd you want to do with him?"

"Same thing we did with Mr. Green. Tie and gag him and we'll carry him down and let him keep Green company." Jung answered.

After removing his gun, with great effort the two Koreans carried Fatso down the stairs, through the West apartment to the back wall, and then through the secret door after unlocking it. They then carried him beside his boss. Trigger's eyes got large and he tried to speak, but the gag prevented it. The men dumped Fatso beside Trigger.

Jung said, "I hope this is the last one. This space is filling up!"

Chapter 13

Friday, October 2, 8:30 am
Sheriff's Office
Harlan, Kentucky

Sheriff Sterling was sitting at his desk completing the security assignments for the 30 national guardsmen and state troopers that were being sent by Governor Atherton and due in his office shortly.

Rosie rang Bert's intercom and said, "Bert, there's a Mr. Austin David calling for you. He says it very important."

Bert thought a minute, and remembered that Austin David was the person that Fatso sometimes got to mind the store when both he and Trigger had to be out. "Okay Rosie, I'll take it."

His phone rang. "This is Bert Sterling, Austin, what can I do for you?"

Austin replied, "Sheriff, this could be nothing, but I thought I'd better tell you anyway. Mrs. Cavanaugh came over to the grocery right after it was suppose to open this morning. I guess she got here about 8:05. But the store was locked up. She knew Fatso always opened a little before 8, so she pulled out her cell phone and tried to call him, but he didn't answer. She then called me and I rushed right over to the store. I looked around inside and couldn't see any trace of Fatso or Trigger. That's extremely unlike them to just leave the store unattended. I don't think it's ever happened before. So I thought I'd better report it to you. Have you heard anything from them?"

Bert replied, "Well, as you know, Fatso couldn't locate Trigger yesterday. I think he got you to mind the store while he came into town looking for him. He stopped by my office, but I hadn't seen or heard from Trigger. I wasn't much help. So it now sounds like both Trigger and Fatso are AWOL."

"Sure looks like it," said Austin. "I'm sure they wouldn't have gone somewhere without making arrangements for the store to be open."

"I agree," the sheriff replied. "I think I'll tell all my deputies to be on the lookout for either of them or their cars. As you know, the festival is kicking off this afternoon and the town will be swamped, but we'll do the best we can do. Can you stay at the store for the day?"

Austin said, "Yeah, I'll stay here, and I'll let you know if I hear anything. Please do the same."

"I sure will Austin. Thanks for letting me know. You take care," replied the sheriff. He hung up the phone and thought, *Now we've got both Trigger and Fatso missing. I'd bet the farm that the MIK guys have something to do with it, but for the time being the only thing I can do is notify all my deputies.*

The intercom buzzed again and Rosie said, "Sheriff, there's a whole army of military and police out here. You better come talk with em."

Bert said, "Be right out, Rosie." He stood, grabbed the stack of papers, and started toward the reception area.

There weren't enough chairs for 30 people in the reception area. A few were seated and the rest were standing about. Two of the state troopers were playing with Preacher Puss. Bert said, "Gentlemen, I'm Sheriff Bert Sterling and I'm delighted to have you here to help us with security for our festival. You've already met my deputy Rosie Cain. And I see at least a couple of you are getting acquainted with our honorary deputy Preacher Puss." Bert chuckled, then pointed toward Deputy Kyle Potter and said, "And that fellow seated there at his desk is my Chief

Deputy Kyle Potter." All 30 nodded and smiled. One of the national guard said, "Sheriff, I'm Captain Silvers. I know I speak for everyone here in saying we're delighted to be of service. The annual festival here enjoys a great reputation and brings folks to Harlan from everywhere. We're honored to be asked to help."

Bert grinned and replied, "Thank you so much Captain Silvers, and thanks to each one of you men."

There were a few loud giggles. Bert looked and saw that three of the National Guard soldiers were female. He laughed and said, "Oh, pardon me. I'm really sorry, ladies, I didn't see you. Let me rephrase that to say we thank each of you men and women!"

All laughed. Bert then said, "I have information and assignment sheets here for each of you. All the assignments will be at random. There are 5 of you assigned to the Seibert Memorial Building to guard the anchor crosses. And there are two shifts....so that takes care of 10. The remaining 20 are assigned to locations around town. The sheets I'm passing out have a map and shows your assigned spot and additional instructions. You'll likely run into a lot of city police, directed by Chief Asher, and several of my deputies. If you don't have any questions I'll ask Deputy Potter to go out with you and help get you all located. My cell number is on the sheets, and I understand you each have cell phones. Please give me a call if you have any questions or if anything pops up that needs attention. Again, thanks so much for all you help."

Kyle stood and went to the door. He held it open while everyone walked out.

Rosie grinned, looked at Bert and said, "Sure glad I didn't have to serve coffee!"

Bert grinned and said, "I thought about it....but then thought better!"

Bert and Rosie then heard the sound of a helicopter. Bert said, "I'm sure that noise is Randy Peters bringing the anchor crosses in the state police helicopter. I better get up to the roof to meet em." He started trotting out the door to the sheriff's department, around the corner of the court house, and into the court house main entrance facing Central Street. Rather than take the elevator he started bounding up the stairs. The roof was four levels up. When he pushed open the roof door to the helipad a great rush of wind hit his face. He looked out and saw the helicopter was just touching down. He waited at the door until the engines were turned off and all the blades stopped turning. The chopper's side door opened and Dr. Randy Peters jumped out carrying a brief case that Bert knew contained the priceless artifacts.

Bert walked over to Randy, shook hands, and said, "Welcome once again to Harlan, my friend. I trust you had a quick and uneventful journey?"

Randy said, "Yeah, it was a smooth and short ride. It's good to be here again."

Three uniformed state police jumped out of the chopper behind Randy and introduced themselves to the sheriff. The five men then began walking to the Seibert Memorial Building.

Upon arrival Bert unlocked the entrance door. Once inside Randy placed his brief case on a table and withdrew the golden anchor crosses. Each was enclosed in a clear plastic case with its name engraved. Inside the memorial there is a large center aisle. Plexiglas enclosures are on both sides of the aisle. Each enclosure runs the length of the building and was designed to house three anchor crosses. Only at festival time each year are the artifacts actually on display. The rest of the time there are simply photographs of them and information describing their history and significance. Each enclosure has three locked, hinged doors to enabled access. The locks are really not designed for security, because when the anchor crosses are on display there are always three armed guards inside and two outside, one at the entrance and one at the exit.

The enclosure locks just prevent any potential robber from quickly opening the display doors.

Randy pulled out a master key that opened the locks on all the enclosure display doors. He unlocked the three on the right, or east side, and then the three on the left, or west side. He then opened all the display doors and carefully placed each anchor cross in its display cradle inside the enclosure. Spot lights fully illuminated each artifact.

He then smiled at Bert and said, "Well, I think that's it. They're all ready for viewing starting this afternoon. I think I'm going to head over to Creech Cafe and try to talk Fred out of a cup of coffee. I bet he's getting all boned up for his welcome speech at 1 o'clock."

"Yeah, I'm sure he is. And I'm sure he'll welcome seeing you and knowing the anchor crosses are all safely delivered," Bert said. "I've got to get back to my office, Randy. Hopefully I'll see you at the opening ceremony."

As the five men left they spoke with each of the five guards that had arrived. Three guards went inside the memorial. The other two went to their outside stations at the front entrance and back exit. The doors were locked until the start of the festival.

Bert and Randy said their goodbyes to the troopers heading back to the helicopter. Randy crossed Central

Street toward Creech's. As Bert walked toward his office he looked at his watch. It was 11:30 am.

• • •

Bert was again sitting at his desk doing paper work. His cell phone rang. He answered it, "This is sheriff Sterling."

It was Deputy Simpson Brown, "Sheriff, I've located those two vehicles. I'm behind the post office. The pickup truck belonging to Maggard's Grocery is parked here beside Trigger Green's car."

Bert said, "Great. Good work, Simpson. I don't suppose there's any sign of Trigger or Fatso."

"Nope," Simpson replied. "I've walked into the post office and all around the area. No luck. Just their vehicles."

"I'm on my way. Just wait there, it shouldn't be more than 5 minutes."

"Will do, boss," replied Simpson.

• • •

Bert and Simpson began the walk from the post office to the old drug store. Bert said, "We have no legal right to search their place, but I thought maybe the sight of the two of us might shake em up. I'd bet the farm that Trigger and Fatso are somewhere in that building."

The two lawmen walked in the entrance door without knocking. Bob Rehsa shouted to them, "Hey guys. Come right in. Bud just went to the john....he'll be back shortly. Can I help you?"

Bert said, "Simpson and I just wanted to pay another quick social visit. We were walking in the area checking everything before the festival opening and just thought we'd say hi."

Bob said, "Yeah, all the activities get underway in just over an hour. Bud and I hope we can take some of it in."

Just then the basement door opened and Jung walked through the door. He saw Bob and the two lawmen standing there and turned pale. He said, "What is it this time?"

Bert smiled and said, "Just stopped in to say hi. But I did have one question for you guys. Both Fatso Chapel and Trigger Green have been reported missing. And we just located their cars parked behind the post office. Did they stop in here, or have you seen them anywhere?"

Bud joined his brother, and after greeting Bert and Simpson he said, "No, I haven't seen em. Have you Bob?"

Bob shook his head and said, "I have not. I sure hope they're okay. They're really good guys."

The lawmen and the brothers then looked at Jung. The color had not returned to his face. He said, "Why would you think we might have seen them?"

"No good reason, Mr. Jung," Bert said. "Just that their cars were parked close by and we knew the brothers here knew them and that you had met them when you first arrived in town. Just thought they might have had some business here."

"No," said Jung. "Now if you'll pardon us we need to get back to work."

Simpson and Bert nodded. Bert said, "Sure. But I'd appreciate it if you'd keep your eyes open and let me know if you see them."

Jung nodded. Bud said, "Absolutely, Bert. You can count on us."

"Okay," Bert said as the two of them turned to leave. "And I hope you find the time to attend some of ACFesV."

Jung, Bob, and Bud nodded. The lawmen left.

●●●

Same Day, 12:45 pm

Downtown

Harlan, Kentucky

Mayor Knapp walked briskly out of Creech Cafe headed toward the platform that had been erected on the Court House steps. He had a folder in his right hand. The entire downtown area had been closed off to traffic. Vendors of all kinds were set up in the streets. Some selling food, others various novelties. Downtown was packed with people. Fred saw several of the national guard and state troopers positioned around the court house. He looked over toward the Seibert Memorial and was pleased to see the guards stationed outside. He knew there were three more inside. It would open to the public very shortly. As he approached the court house platform he was comforted to see all that were supposed to be there already seated on stage. He walked up the platform stairs, turned, and with a big grin waved at the huge audience. He then walked along the line of seated dignitaries and participants, shaking hands and chatting briefly with each one. Finally, he walked up to the podium, opened his folder, and after introducing everyone on stage started his welcoming speech. It was exactly 1 pm.

●●●

Same Day, 6 pm

Creech Cafe

Harlan, Kentucky

Creech's was packed. There was not an empty table or stool, and several folks were at the front waiting to be seated. Fred had told Bennie to hold a table in the very back for their meeting at 6 pm. In addition to the mayor, Dr. Randy Peters, Deputy Potter, and sheriff Sterling had just finished their dinner and were enjoying coffee.

With a really big smile Fred said, "Boys, the day was a huge success. All the speeches and programs came off very good. There's been a long line at the Memorial all day to view the anchor crosses, and it's still out there. No problems have been reported with security. Chief Asher and his men tell me that traffic was handled without incident..... but it was very heavy. And just look at this crowd here in my modest little cafe." Fred spread his hands toward his customers.

Dr. Randy Peters said, "Yeah, Fred, it all seemed to come off extremely well, thanks to you and the rest of the planning committee. We've still got two more days to go, but we're certainly off to a great start. I was so pleased to see all the interest in viewing the anchor crosses. I spent a lot of time there at the Memorial today answering questions for folks." He looked at Kyle and said, "Deputy Potter, you sure did start something when you found that first one."

Kyle replied, "I had no idea what I had found. But it sure turned out mighty good."

Bert said, "The festival is just great, but I'm very, very concerned about Trigger and Fatso. I just know those Koreans have them, or at least know something. But without some proof my hands are tied. Finding their cars that close to the old drug store building sealed it for me. But without a search warrant there's nothing we can do."

"We've just got to think positive and hope that the good Lord will keep them safe and deliver them soon," Fred replied.

Kyle said, "We've sure got a full day tomorrow, so I'm going to suggest we all head home early and try and get some rest."

Randy, Kyle, and Bert all just stared at Fred. Finally the mayor said with a grin, "I bet you're wanting a good story to travel on."

All three nodded agreement.

Fred started, "Here's the latest. I just heard it this afternoon. There were these two elderly ladies that had been lifelong friends. Over the years they had done everything together.

Now in their later years they got together a couple of times a week, usually to play cards. One day while they were playing cards one looked at the other and asked that she not get mad at her for the question she was about to ask, and then she asked the other one her name. She said she had thought and thought but just couldn't remember it. Her lifelong friend just stared at her for about three minutes and then asked, how soon do you need to know?"

The four stood laughing. Fred motioned to four people waiting on a table to come on back.

• • •

Same Day, 8 pm
Old Drug Store Building
Harlan, Kentucky

The 10 were once again gathered for a meeting on the first floor of the old drug store building. Jung pointed out the front window toward the Seibert Memorial Building across the street and said, "Look at that line of people waiting to see the artifacts. Just think, guys, tomorrow night they'll be ours!"

Everyone was silent for a moment, and then Park said, "I took our prisoners some water and a few crackers. I hope that was okay."

Jung replied, "Softie! Yeah, as long as you put the gags back on nice and tight. We sure don't want them making any noise."

"I did," replied Park.

Jung said, "I told the Rehea brothers to take tomorrow off, so we'll not see them again. And unless one of you tells me different, everything is all set for our missions tomorrow night, so I suggest we all go to the festival tomorrow and enjoy ourselves."

The other 9 nodded agreement and started clapping.

Jung said, "Hold it down. We don't want to draw attention. Have fun tomorrow, but be back here no later than 8 pm. Just as soon as they close the Memorial tomorrow night my group will head for the tunnel and start drilling the hole in the bottom of the floor. Rhee, you and Choe will leave for the Slusher farm at 10:30, and Yi and Park will leave here around midnight to go to the sheriff's office. Correct?"

The four nodded approval. Jung then said, "So I'll send our last report from Harlan to our Supreme Leader tomorrow morning. I'm sure he'll be excited and pleased. You are dismissed....get a good night's rest."

Chapter 14

Saturday, October 3, 10:30 am

Downtown

Harlan, Kentucky

Fred was mingling through the crowd, stopping to shake hands and chat with folks every few steps. He was all smiles. He was in his element. Suddenly he heard, "Mr. Mayor, Mr. Mayor, could I have a minute?"

He turned toward the voice and saw Lexington television station WKYT's anchor Barbara Clark trying to reach him. She was trailed by a cameraman. When they reached the mayor she said, "Mayor Knapp, it is so good to see you once again. And what a wonderful turnout you have for this years festival. Would you be so kind as to allow me a short interview?"

The cameraman started recording. Fred beamed, shook hands with Barbara, and said, "Barbara, how good to have you here again this year. Of course, I'd be delighted to talk with you."

The interview continued for another five minutes or so. Fred waxed elegantly.

● ● ●

Dr. Randy Peters was inside the Seibert Memorial answering questions about the anchor crosses. The line to get in the building stretched half way around the court house property. Randy looked toward the entrance after chatting for a minute with a very nice lady. He saw Jon Shell walking in with two cameras strapped across his neck. Jon lives in Lexington, and is Kentucky's leading photographer. Randy and Jon were friends. Randy waved toward Jon and shouted, "Hey Jon. Come over here."

Jon walked over to Randy with a smile. "Dr. Peters, I sort of thought I might find you here. Anywhere these beautiful anchor crosses are located, there you find Randy Peters."

Randy beamed and replied, "I do have a fondness for them. Are you getting lots of good pictures?"

"Sure are. I've been wondering around all through town. So many interesting things to photograph at this festival. But now I'm here to photograph the stars, those beautiful golden anchor crosses. You think I could get a few shots of you with them?"

"Absolutely, Jon, I would be greatly honored. As a matter of fact, let me get one out of the enclosure and hold it up. You could get a lot better picture that way."

"Great," replied Jon.

Randy then unlocked the Plexiglas door to the Seibert Anchor Cross. After opening the door he reached in and removed the artifact from its cradle and then held it up beside his face. The three security guards inside the building all walked over and moved the fascinated visitors back away from Jon and Randy, making room for the photograph.

Jon took 4 or 5 shots of Randy holding the golden anchor cross. He then said, "Thanks so much Randy. I think I've got some great ones."

"You are more than welcome, my friend," Randy said as he replaced the artifact back in its cradle in the enclosure and closed and locked its door.

Jon then walked around inside taking additional pictures of people viewing the anchor crosses. He and Randy continued to chat for a while.

● ● ●

One group of musicians was singing and playing from the stage at the court house steps. Several other groups and bands were playing at various locations throughout the downtown area. Music filled the air. It was a glorious October morning. Not hot, not cold. Just perfect. And the sun beamed brightly. People walking about seemed to be greatly enjoying ACFesV.

It was quite a sight to see. Stood out like a sore thumb. The 10 North Koreans were walking together down Main Street. Trailing about a half block behind them were the two G-Men, Cody Short and Sammy King. The two agents were probably the only men in Harlan County wearing suits and ties. Sheriff Sterling was following the procession too. He was across the street from the G-Men. The sheriff had staked out the old drug store building, thinking he might see something suspicious, or even perhaps Trigger or Fatso. Unknown to him was that the G-Men were also watching the building. When the MIK guys walked out and turned left onto 1st Street the sheriff and the G-Men trailed behind. They all walked up to Mound Street, turned left and went down to Main, turned left again and were now approaching Central Street. The procession turned left onto Central Street and when they got back to the old drug store they crossed the street and got in the line waiting to go into the Seibert Memorial. The G-Men and the sheriff both walked to the Memorial exit.

As he saw Cody and Sammy walking up Bert said, "Hey guys. I bet we've all been following the same group."

Cody said, "Yeah, and now that it looks like they're getting ready to go into the Memorial we just might see some action. You think they might try something right here with all the security and people around?"

Bert shrugged his shoulders and said, "I just don't know. But I figure it's worth checking out."

The three then turned to the security guard that was positioned at the Memorial Building exit and showed him their credentials. They explained to him that when the Asian-looking guys got inside the Memorial they wanted to enter from the exit. He agreed. Bert then asked the guard if he would please call the guards inside the building to let them know what was going to happen. He agreed, and did.

Bert watched the line from around the back corner of the Memorial. It was another 45 minutes before the first of the MIK guys got to the entrance. He then watched until the tenth entered and then asked the guard to please let them enter the exit.

As they entered the sheriff went on one side and the two G-Men on the other. They all stayed close to the exit, just watching the MIK guys looking at the anchor crosses along with other viewers. The Koreans moved swiftly through the Memorial. Jung was leading the group. As he neared the exit he saw the sheriff watching him.

He walked over to Bert and said, "Lovely artifacts. Are you playing guard here today?"

Bert smiled and said, "Just watching the crowd. You guys take the day off?"

"Certainly," Jung replied. "We didn't want to miss the festival."

Bert nodded. The other 9 followed Jung closely as they left the building. Bert looked across the aisle toward the G-Men and shrugged. He then exited to follow the Koreans. Cody and Sammy were close behind.

When they got out of the Memorial the MIK guys walked up Central Street toward the Court House entrance. They found space on one of the low concrete walls that circle the property, and all sat on it and listened to the music being performed from the Court House stage. Bert, Cody, and Sammy all walked across Central Street and leaned against a building while watching the Koreans.

After about an hour the 10 all stood up, and then started to disperse in different directions. Some went to food venders and purchased something to eat. Some walked up closer to the performers on the stage, some walked down 1st Street looking at each vender's offerings, and a couple, Yi and Park, just stretched and then sat back down on the concrete wall to listen to more of the music.

Bert looked at Cody and Sammy and shrugged his shoulders. "Beats me. If they're up to something I sure don't know what it is."

Sammy said, "Yeah. Can't arrest them for enjoying the festival."

The three continued to watch.

After a few minutes Bert saw Rosie walking down the sidewalk with Preacher Puss on a leash. All of his deputies were here working security for the festival. He figured Rosie was just out for a break while another deputy covered for her in the office. A big smile formed on his face as he watched people stop her to chat and then reach down and pet the cat. He could tell even from this distance that Preacher Puss was greatly enjoying her stroll and getting all the attention. After several stops the deputy and cat came to where Yi and Park were sitting. They were facing away from the sidewalk, toward the Court House stage enjoying the music.

Suddenly Preacher Puss lunged strongly toward Yi. She jumped, and with claws extended, landed on the back of his neck. He screamed and reached up with both hands to grab the cat. He pulled her loose. She then immediately jumped on Park, who had turned facing her. She landed on his left arm about midway between hand and elbow, and her claws again dug in deeply. Park screamed loudly. Yi had stood up and was trying to grab the cat away from Park, but Preacher Puss would not let go. Blood was running down Yi's neck and down Park's arm.

Rosie pulled hard on the cat's leash and screamed, "Preacher Puss, you let go. You behave yourself." The cat obeyed, fell to the ground, and walked beside Rosie.

Rosie looked at the two men and said, "Guys, I'm awfully sorry. My cat has never attacked anyone that way before. You didn't provoke her at all. I just don't understand it." She then pulled a Kleenex from her pocket and tried to start wiping the blood from Park's arm.

Bert, having witnessed the entire encounter, came running up and pulled Rosie back from the men. Preacher Puss stayed at Rosie's feet. Bert said, "Stay back, Rosie, I'll handle this. You just hang onto our cat."

Rosie said, "But Bert, these men didn't do anything. Preacher Puss just attacked them."

Bert looked at the bandaged right wrist of Yi and said, "I think the cat knew what she was doing. I think these are the two men that kidnapped her and then tried to kill me!"

Yi and Park stood frozen looking at the sheriff. Yi said, "You prove that, Mr. Sheriff."

Park said, "Yeah, we don't know what you're talking about."

Bert said to Rosie, "You take Preacher Puss and get back to the office. I'll take care of these two." Rosie reached down and gathered the cat up in her arms, nodded to Bert, and started walking back to her office.

The sheriff then looked at Yi and Park and said, "Unfortunately, you are right. I cannot prove it. But you both know, and now I know, that you're the guilty ones. I have to let you go for now, but there'll be another time. That I can promise you."

Yi was holding his right hand over the wound on the back of his neck. Park was holding Rosie's Kleenex on his arm. Blood was still coming from both wounds. The two men started walking toward the old drug store building.

A crowd of people had gathered around watching the cat attacks. Bert turned to them and said, "Okay people, this show's over, get back to the festival." They slowly began to disperse.

Cody and Sammy walked up to Bert. Cody said, "Anyway you'd allow the federal government to borrow Preacher Puss for a few months to try and understand how we could replicate her? I've never seen anything like that before. She absolutely knew those were the two men that tried to kill you."

Bert smiled and said, "No, you can't have her. I know everything that goes to Washington never comes back! But you're absolutely correct, those were the guilty guys and she knew it. At least they have a few fresh wounds, and Preacher Puss and I feel real good about that!"

Sammy said, "You should, sheriff. I guess Cody and I will leave you now and go trail some of the other Koreans. Call if you need us."

Bert said, "Thanks guys. Sure will." As he then turned and started to walk back to his office he saw Carolyn Potter running up to him.

She said, "Bert, I saw the crowd over her. Are you okay?"

"I'm fine, honey. As a matter of fact, I'm real fine. Ole Preacher Puss just did her stuff again on two bad guys." He smiled, and then told her what happened.

She gave him a kiss and said, "I'm so pleased you're okay. Are we still on for church tomorrow morning?

"You bet we are," he said as he gave her a pat on the arm. "You go enjoy the festival for the rest of the day and I'll see you tomorrow at church." They each then walked their separate ways.

Chapter 15

Saturday, October 3, 8 pm

Old Drug Store Building

Harlan, Kentucky

Jung, seated with the other 9 around the makeshift table on the first floor, stared at General Yi and Park. He said, "Our entire mission came very close to failing this afternoon due to you two. The sheriff and every other law enforcement person in Harlan County now know about us. And the Supreme Leader is not going to appreciate this."

Yi said, "General Jung, we simply couldn't help what happened. All we were doing was sitting listening to the music when that woman deputy and her pussycat came strolling by behind our backs. There was nothing we could have done. That cat just somehow sensed us and attacked.

In a few more hours our missions will be complete and we'll be out of here and it won't matter."

Park nodded agreement.

"It's a good thing," replied Jung. "Just look at yourselves....all taped up like you've been wounded in battle. And just because of a crazy pussycat."

Jung continued, "But you are right about one thing, we should be headed back to Pyongyang in just a matter of hours. Is everyone clear on the missions tonight?"

All nodded.

"Good. Then I'll stay here on the first floor and watch the Memorial building. When they close for the night I'll gather the rest of my team and we'll get started on our mission. The rest of you might wish to get a nap.... it's going to be a long night.

● ● ●

Same Day, 9 pm
Old Drug Store Building
Harlan, Kentucky

General Jung ran upstairs and yelled to his crew, "Okay men, they just closed the Memorial. Let's get cracking."

The six soldiers walked down to the basement and through the door in the false back wall of the West apartment.

Trigger and Fatso both tried to talk to them, but the gags were too tight to allow it. The soldiers passed the prisoners carrying their equipment into the tunnel. One by one they crawled, pushing their equipment in front of them.

They finally reached the vertical shaft running up to the bottom of the Memorial floor. General Jung positioned the miner on the vertical hydraulic cylinder that, when actuated, would raise the miner up to contact the concrete floor. They had changed the head on the miner such that it now had new, sharp teeth to cut through the concrete slab. Jung then pushed the appropriate button on the miner to set it's rotary speed to the slowest setting. Next he started the motor on the vertical hydraulic cylinder. The miner started it's slow rise up to the bottom of the Memorial floor. When the teeth touched the concrete they started slowly turning and cutting a two foot hole in the floor. It would take about two hours to complete its job. The men backed themselves out of the tunnel to wait. It was 9:45 pm.

●●●

Same Day, 10:30 pm
Old Drug Store Building
Harlan, Kentucky

General Rhee and Choe Chae-yeong walked out the front door headed to their car. Choe was carrying a large box. When they reached the car Rhee unlocked the trunk and they together carefully placed the box in it. They then got in the car and began the drive to the Slusher farm.

After about 15 minutes they turned left off highway 119 onto the road that would take them to the farm. When they got almost to the guard gate, but still out of site of it, Rhee stopped the car. Choe got out with the baseball bat in his hand. He then walked behind the car as it proceeded toward the gate.

George noticed the headlights coming up the road toward his gate. He thought, *it's almost 11 o'clock. The brothers aren't expecting anyone tonight that I know of. Wonder who it could be?*

The car pulled beside the guard gate. George opened the window and said, "May I help you?"

General Rhee replied with a smile, "Oh yes, I'm terribly sorry to bother you, but I must have taken the wrong road. Could you possibly give me directions?"

"Sure," George said, "where do you want to go?"

The baseball bat struck George's head just as he asked the question. He slumped to the floor unconscious. Choe pulled the cloth and duct tape from his back pocket. He stuffed the cloth in George's mouth and then wrapped the duct tape a couple of loops around his head, covering his mouth. He then turned George on his stomach and pulled his arms behind his back. He put several loops of duct tape around his wrists and then did the same to his feet. He stood up and said, "He's all secure, Rhee. I'll hit the button to open the gate and be right there with you."

"Hurry," General Rhee replied.

The gate opened. Choe got in the car, and they drove into the Slusher brothers' property. Rhee turned his headlights off. The moon plus some driveway lights enabled them to see the way. As they emerged from the trees they spotted the home straight ahead. Rather than drive up in the front they took a side road that circled around to the back. Rhee spotted the gardening shed that was attached to the house. He pulled the car as close as possible to it and turned off the motor. They got out and walked around to the back of the car. Not a sound could be heard. They quietly removed the large wooden box from the trunk and started walking toward the shed. Suddenly they noticed a line of cats sitting around the shed door watching them. They carefully put the box down on the ground.

Choe looked at Rhee and quietly said, "Wonder if any of those guys are related to the sheriff's cat?"

"I sure hope not," Rhee whispered.

He then walked up to the shed, shooed the cats away, opened the door and returned to the box. The two carefully lifted and carried it inside the shed. They placed it up against the back wall of the house and then opened the top of the box. Choe held a flashlight while Rhee bent over and slowly and carefully set the timer on the bomb. The red digital numbers corresponding to the detonation time registered 1:00 am. Similar numbers on the current time clock indicated 11:35 pm.

After setting the bomb Rhee stood up and whispered, "That's it. All ready to go. Let's get out of here."

The two crept back toward their car, using their feet to push cats out of the way. They shut the shed door quietly and then got in the car. Rhee started it and they pulled around the house headed back down the driveway.

Rhee said, "I feel relieved. I was really worried that someone might hear our car, but I guess that home has good insulation."

They got to the guard gate. Rhee stopped and said, "Choe, look in there and make sure George is still all secure."

Choe jumped out of the car, walked to the guard house window and looked in. He saw George still prone with hands and feet secured with the duct tape. He turned, jumped back in the car, and said, "He's good. Let's get to Harlan!"

The car sped off down the drive. It was 11:45 pm.

● ● ●

Same Day, Same Time
Old Drug Store Building
Harlan, Kentucky

Jung looked at his watch. He said, "Okay guys, we should now have a hole in the middle of the Memorial floor. Let's go grab those anchor crosses."

All smiled and nodded agreement. They again passed Trigger and Fatso as they entered the tunnel. After crawling for about 10 minutes they reached the vertical shaft going up to the Memorial. Pieces of concrete had to first be shoved forward into the tunnel in a space they had made for that purpose. Then they reversed the motor on the hydraulic cylinder and lowered the miner. It took another 15 minutes to disengage the two and then move them into the same space where the concrete pieces had been shoved. They were now ready to climb the tunnel wall up to the Seibert Memorial Building floor. To do this they had to use their hands to dig out toe steps in the sides of the dirt tunnel wall. They then started the trip up into the Memorial. Jung led the way. When his head got to the top he stopped and carefully listened to see if he could hear anything. All was quiet. He proceeded up through the hole, followed by the other 5 men. When they were all in the building each removed a small metal blade they used to open the locks on the Plexiglas enclosure doors. Fortunately, the spot lights shining on the artifacts were left on.....so they didn't have to use their flashlights. Each man then reached through their door and removed an anchor cross from its cradle. They looked in amazement at the startlingly beautiful golden artifacts. Each then placed the one they were holding in a pocket and the procession of 6 began going back down the tunnel hole in the middle of the building. In another 15 minutes they exited through the back wall of the old drug store building and then walked up to the first floor. It was 12:45 am

• • •

General Rhee and Choe were waiting for Jung and his crew when they arrived back on the first floor. Rhee said with a smile, "Welcome, welcome, welcome. I bet you guys each have one of those beautiful golden anchor crosses."

Each of the six reached in his pocket and pulled out an anchor cross. They held them high in the air with their left hand, and saluted with their right. There was a big smile on everyone's face.

General Jung looked at Rhee and Choe and asked, "Did you achieve your mission?"

They both nodded vigorously, smiled, looked at their watches and Rhee said, "In exactly 10 minutes the ten deserters and the others at the farm will be gone, including a lot of cats. Our mission went perfectly."

Jung replied, "Wonderful. I assume Yi and Park are finishing their mission and should be back any time now. Everyone grab your luggage and be ready to head home as soon as they get here."

• • •

About an Hour Earlier
Old Drug Store Building
Harlan, Kentucky

General Yi looked at his watch. He said, "Okay Park, by the time we get there the second shift should be gone. Lets head to the sheriff's office."

Park grabbed a backpack and a flashlight. Yi picked up a flashlight and small tool kit. They left headed for the sheriff's office.

Outside they started walking, first across Central Street and then onto the Court House property. They walked beside the Seibert Memorial and noticed the two guards, one at the exit and another at the entrance. There were still lots of festival attendees milling about outside so their presence went unnoticed. As they were getting ready to pass by the stage set up on the Court House steps two Harlan City Police appeared in front of them from around the corner. They were engaged in conversation and weren't looking ahead. Yi and Park ducked under the stage to hide from them. When the policemen got to the other corner of the stage, they decided to have a seat on the steps and continue their conversation. From where they sat they could not see the two Koreans under the stage on the other side. The policemen each then lit a cigarette and started telling jokes while remaining seated. This went on for about 30 minutes.

Yi looked at Park and whispered, "Surely they'll leave soon. We need to get on with it."

Park nodded.

A couple of minutes later one of the cops said, "You ready to get going?"

The other nodded. They stood and walked to Central Street and turned west walking down the sidewalk.

"Okay," Yi said. "The coast is clear, let's get to the back door."

The two soldiers resumed their mission. They arrived at the back door to the sheriff's office. Yi held his flashlight while Park used a tool to open the door. They walked inside, closed the door behind them, and headed into the sheriff's office. They got to the door going from his office into the reception area. Since the office had no windows, Park flipped a light switch to turn on the lights. He then took off his backpack, placed it on the floor, and very carefully removed the bomb assembly and using about half a roll of duct tape fastened it to the floor just inside the door. Yi then handed him the trip-wire assembly. Using a screw driver he fastened one end of it to the inside bottom of the door and the other end to the bomb detonator. He looked at Yi and said, "I think that's it. When the sheriff attempts to open that door he and everyone in here will be blown to smithereens."

Yi smiled and said, "Yeah. Including that damn cat."

Park nodded, grinned, and said, "You bet!"

Yi said, "Mission accomplished. Let's get out of here!"

● ● ●

Sunday, October 4, 1 am
Old Drug Store Building
Harlan, Kentucky

General Jung looked at his watch with a worried frown, "They should have been here by now."

The other 7 nodded agreement. Rhee said, "Well, the good news is that the deserters and their friends should now be history." All smiled and nodded.

The door opened and in walked Yi and Park. Jung said, "We were worried about you two. What took so long?"

Yi said, "No problem. Mission accomplished. We just had to hide for a half hour while two city policemen took a break. Otherwise, everything went exactly as planned. When Sheriff Sterling opens his office door on Monday morning he, his damned cat, and anyone else in the office will be eliminated."

Jung patted Yi and Park on their backs. He grinned and said, "Wonderful news. You two go grab your luggage. We've already loaded ours. It's time to head home..... missions accomplished!"

● ● ●

One Hour Earlier, Midnight
Slusher Brothers Farm
Harlan County, Kentucky

George felt like he'd been run over by a freight train. His head was splitting! He was about to strangle from something in his mouth, and he couldn't move his hands or feet. And then he remembered what happened. That guy that pulled up in the car and said he was lost. Someone with him must have busted me over the head. He looked around the floor and saw the baseball bat. Yep, he thought, that's exactly what happened. And then panic set in. He realized those bad guys had likely entered the farm to harm or kill everyone there. He had to call the police. He just had to.

He started twisting his hands. He could see the duct tape around his feet. He assumed his hands were likely restrained the same way. He twisted his hands hard....no luck. They were well taped.

Then he remembered that he'd laid a real sharp hand sickle over in the corner. He had been using it yesterday to clear some weeds around the guard shack. He looked and saw it. He started wiggling his way over to it. After a few minutes he arrived beside it. He rolled on his side such that his hands were beside the sickle. Fortunately for him, the sickle was on one of a pair of old shoes he kept there in the corner. It's sharp blade was pointed up at about a 45 degree angle. He wiggled around until he could feel the blade, and then moved his taped hands over it and started to saw the tape loose. It didn't take long. Hands free he removed the tape over his mouth, pulled out the cloth gag, and then reached down and untapped his feet. He jumped up and reached in his pocket for his cell phone. He had sheriff Sterling on its speed dial.

Bert rolled over and grabbed the ringing phone resting on the table beside his bed, "Sheriff Sterling,"

"Bert, this is George at the Slusher farm. We've got a big emergency here. A couple of guys knocked me out and entered the farm. I don't have any idea what they're up to, but I'm pretty sure it's bad. I don't know if they're still in there or not. I'm headed there just as soon as I hang up. You need to get a bunch of cops over here asap. And it might not be a bad idea to bring a bomb smelling dog. It's uncertain what they're up to. But hurry."

Bert jumped up out of bed and said, "You be careful, George. We're on it."

George rubbed his aching head as he trotted around to the back of the guard building and got in his car. He raced to the house, pulled up in the front driveway, jumped out and ran to the door. He stuck his key in the lock and entered the house. He then yelled at the top of his lungs, "EVERYONE WAKE UP. ITS AN EMERGENCY. GET OUT OF THIS HOUSE RIGHT NOW."

He then started running from one bedroom to another beating on the doors. Lights started turning on all over the house. People started coming out into the hallways.

"Get out. Quick. Quick. Get out of the house, I think there might be a bomb getting ready to explode. Get out now. Forget getting dressed!"

Everyone started rushing for the door. Finally George counted 14 of them standing out in the front yard. He knew they were all out. He then ran out the door and told them to all move way back from the house and wait for the police to arrive. They did as told.

George was then explaining everything to the group when sirens could be heard coming their way. In a couple of minutes four emergency vehicles appeared with flashing lights. The lead car was Sheriff Sterling. He jumped out and ran up to George and said, "Is everyone out?"

George smiled and said, "Yes sir, all accounted for, sheriff."

They heard a dog bark loudly and saw a Kentucky State Trooper trailing the dog on a leash. They were running for the house. Kyle Potter and Mousy Giles next appeared. Kyle asked Bert, "What can we do?"

He said, "George thinks there could be a bomb planted somewhere around the house. Most likely on the outside. We better help the trooper and his dog hunt for it."

The three lawmen started running for the house. The trooper and dog had gone around to the right, so Bert and his deputies headed left around the house. They met up in the back. The dog was going nuts jumping up and down and barking at the door to the gardening shed.

The trooper waved the three from the sheriff's office back. He said, "You guys standoff. If there's a bomb in there it could be a big one. Big Nose here and I will check it out."

With the dog, Big Nose, the trooper opened the shed door and entered. Big Nose immediately ran to the wooden box and continued barking and jumping up and down. The trooper removed the lid on the box and immediately saw the two red digital readouts. One read 1:00 am, the other 12:56 am, and counting. He removed a pair of pliers from his tool belt and very carefully pulled a wire going to the 1:00 am readout. He put the pliers around the wire and clipped it. The two readouts went dark.

He then shouted to the sheriff and deputies, "How about a hand in here." All three came running.

They carried the bomb away from the house into the field and sat it down.

Bert smiled at the trooper and said, "Friend, you and ole Big Nose sure do good work!"

The trooper smiled back, petted his dog, and said, "We try. Just glad we were able to locate it in time. We only had a couple of minutes left. And it was a huge bomb. Likely would have leveled the house." The trooper took the dog back around to his cruiser. They got in and pulled it around to the back of the house and loaded up the defused bomb.

Everyone then walked around to the front of the house to the group still standing there in their pajamas. Bert said, "Okay guys. It's safe to go back in now, we got it. Ole Big Nose sniffed it out with a couple of minutes to spare."

George then told his story to the lawmen, permitting them to complete their reports. Kyle administered first aid and got him all bandaged up. George said he was feeling much better. Gunsmoke and Booger proclaimed him a hero. Then the backslaps, handshakes, hugs, and thanking continued for another fifteen minutes before the lawmen left and the Slusher farm crew returned to bed.

• • •

Same Day, 3 am

Highway 33

Near Tazewell, Tennessee

The Koreans had just turned off highway 25E onto route 33 headed for Knoxville. Jung was driving the car with the van following. Jung had just called Kim Jong-un and reported the success of all their missions.

Jung said, "The Supreme Leader was so happy he could hardly talk. He said to congratulate each of you, and that you would be greatly rewarded upon return. He's planning a huge celebration for next Saturday. He says it will be the largest gathering in the history of North Korea. He said arrangements have been made with Mr. Maggard in Knoxville for us to get some sleep in the same motel we stayed in previously, and then when we feel rested we can begin our journey back to Brunswick, Georgia to meet up with Captain Juan for the return trip back to Havana where his private jet will meet us at the airport. All arrangements have been made."

The four other soldiers in Jung's car cheered and clapped loudly. The celebration was on.

Chapter 16

Sunday, October 4
Seibert Memorial Building
Harlan, Kentucky

Bert got only about 3 hours sleep. By the time he got home and to bed it was close to 3 am. He then had trouble sleeping. He kept thinking about how close all 15 men at the Slusher Farm had come to being killed. And he wondered where Trigger and Fatso were. It was a troubling sleep. He woke a few minutes before 6 and by 6:30 he had arrived at the Seibert Memorial.

As he walked toward the entrance the guard on duty said, "Well good morning Sheriff Sterling. You're stirring mighty early."

Bert replied, "Early bird gets the worm. I just wanted to check a couple of things down here before you open up at 8." He started pulling out his key chain.

"You need me to go in with you, sheriff?"

"No, no. Not necessary," Bert replied as he found the key to the Memorial, placed and turned it in the lock, and opened the door.

The guard said, "You just shout if you need me."

"Will do," Bert replied as he walked inside and closed the door behind him.

His eyes were first drawn to the spotlights shining on the empty cradles where the anchor crosses should have been. His mouth dropped open as he realized they weren't there. The blood drained from his face. He thought, *This cannot be. Those artifacts have been under heavy security since their arrival. They cannot possibly be missing.*

And then he looked down the center aisle. He couldn't believe his eyes when he saw the huge hole in the floor. He walked over to it and looked down. A black hole going down as far as he could see. This simply cannot have happened, he thought. But apparently it had.

He pulled the cell phone from his pocket and hit the speed dial for Pastor Raymond Bell's home. He heard, "Yes, good morning, this is Pastor Bell."

"Raymond," the sheriff said, "we got a problem. Is Randy awake?"

Dr. Randy Peters had been invited to stay again at the home of his friend Raymond Bell while he was visiting in Harlan.

"I think he just got up. Let me get him for you," replied the pastor.

"Thanks, Raymond," Bert said.

In just a few seconds Randy said, "Morning, Bert. Calls at this hour of the morning usually are not good."

"For sure," the sheriff said. "I'm standing in the Memorial. All the anchor crosses are missing, and there's a large hole in the center of the floor."

There was a long pause. Randy then said, "I'll be there in 10 minutes."

"Thanks, do hurry," Bert replied. He replaced the phone in his pocket and pulled the flashlight from off his belt.

He got down on his knees and pointed the flashlight down into the hole. It looked like about 10 feet down he could see the bottom and what looked like a tunnel going off to one side. He noticed dug out places along the sides of the hole where the robbers likely placed their feet to climb and descend.

He heard the door open. Randy Peters entered, shut the door, and trotted over to Bert.

Randy said, "Wow. Hard to believe!"

The sheriff stood up and said, "I'm just so, so sorry, Randy. We had what we thought was super security here, but we sure didn't think about anyone digging a tunnel under the floor. They outsmarted us. But we'll get those anchor crosses back somehow. I just feel terrible!"

Randy patted the sheriff on the shoulder, smiled, and said, "Bert, I have a confession to make."

Bert looked surprised, and said, "You have a confession? I don't understand."

Randy said, "The CIA Director, Max Snell, came to see me and talked me into letting him make duplicates of the anchor crosses. He was very much worried that this might happen, and he didn't want the artifacts to fall into the wrong hands. I was reluctant, because I didn't want to deceive the people coming to view them, but he convinced me it was in the national interest to do it. I reluctantly agreed. He said we should keep it a secret from everyone else so all could think the originals were on display. So whoever stole them just got some beautiful fakes."

Bert looked tremendously relieved. He smiled and said, "Maybe you need to hold me up, Randy. I think I might faint!"

Randy again patted him on the back and said, "You're going to be just fine, Bert. Rest assured the originals are all safe and sound back in Lexington in my vault. Somebody sure went to a lot of trouble to steal the fakes."

"You can say that again," the sheriff said.

They both stood looking down into the hole as Bert beamed his flashlight down it. Bert then handed the flashlight to Randy and said, "Hold this a moment, I'm going to take my jacket off and go down there to see what I can see."

Randy held the flashlight and said, "You be careful."

Bert threw his jacket to the side and took back the flashlight. He got down on all fours and started backwards down the hole, carefully locating each foot slot as he descended. After a few minutes he was standing at the bottom. He shouted up to Randy, "I'm going to crawl down this tunnel to see where it goes. I have my cell phone if I need your help. I'll give you a call when I find the end of the tunnel. In the meantime, don't let any of the guards come into the building to see what's happened. We'll post a notice that the Memorial is closed today due to some safety issue. I don't want anyone to know the anchor crosses are missing, even though they're fake. Okay?"

"Yeah, makes sense to me," Randy replied. "But you be very, very careful, my friend. I'll await your call."

•••

Trigger and Fatso started to hear noises coming from the tunnel. They began getting louder. Although they were too weak to even move, they both were lying with their faces pointing toward the tunnel entrance. They watched expectantly.

A beam of light appeared. Then his head came out. It was covered with dirt, but they immediately recognized Bert. Smiles tugged at their gags. As he moved the flashlight around and it struck his two friends he became overjoyed. He jumped out of the tunnel and ran over to them. He first tore off the tape from around their heads and removed the gags. He could tell they wanted to speak, but were too weak.

He said, "What a sight for sore eyes! Hang in there guys, I'm calling for help right now."

He pulled out his phone, dialed 911, and reported the situation to the operator.

He said, "Help is on the way. Be here very soon." He then took the tape off their hands and feet. They were free. He just hoped they would be okay.

Bert then picked up his phone and dialed Randy. He told him what had happened and asked him to come on over to the old drug store building and he'd meet him at the entrance door. He walked over to the door in the false wall and tried the knob. The deadbolt was locked. He then walked back to the real wall and took a flying leap toward the door and slammed his feet against it with all his might. When they hit the door the hinges broke and the door fell to the apartment floor. He stood and walked through the door. His flashlight revealed a light switch on the wall. He turned on the lights and then headed for the steps up to the first floor. Just before he got to the front door he heard a banging on it. Randy had arrived. He opened the door. The two friends hugged.

They each heard the ambulance at the same time. It was coming down 1st Street with siren screaming. The two walked out on the sidewalk and waved to them as they pulled to the curb. Two EMT's jumped out and followed Bert and Randy down to Trigger and Fatso. They administered first-aid and gave them some water before going back and bringing down two stretchers. Bert and Randy volunteered to help carry them to the ambulance. Their friends were soon inside and on their way to the hospital.

Standing on the corner of Central and 1st Streets Bert and Randy watched the ambulance speed off down Central toward the Harlan by-pass.

Randy looked at Bert, who was covered in dirt, and said with a smile, "Sheriff, if you're planning on going to church this morning I suggest a bath might be in order."

Bert laughed, patted Randy on the back, and said, "I feel like I once did as a kid after playing in the dirt all day. But you are correct, my friend, I'm headed home for a good hot shower and then to meet up with Carolyn at church."

"I'll see you there," Randy replied. "Anything more I can do here?"

Bert thought a moment and said, "Would you mind going back over to the Memorial and tell the guards there's been a problem and the Memorial will be closed today? You could make up a sign with a felt pen and post it on the door. And after locking it up you could let the guards leave.

"Be glad to. I'll see you at church." Randy started walking toward the Memorial.

"Thank you my friend," Bert said. He looked at his watch. It was 7:45. Plenty of time to close up here, get home and cleaned up before the 11 am service.

● ● ●

Same Time
Knoxville, Tennessee

The North Koreans were visiting with Pretty Boy Maggard at his junk yard before going to the motel to get rested up for their trip.

When they arrived at the junk yard Pretty Boy was waiting for them. The three generals got out of their vehicles and went into the office. General Jung asked Pretty Boy if he had heard anything on the news about a big explosion last night in Harlan County that killed 15 people. He said no.

Jung then said, "Could we turn on your television and catch the news at 8 am. I would like to see if they say anything about the explosion."

"Sure," said Pretty Boy. He reached for the remote and turned on the small television that sat on a cabinet next to the wall. "I'll put it on the Hazard, Kentucky station, WYMT. They carry any Eastern Kentucky news."

"Thank you," Jung replied. The three generals pulled up chairs and watched.

Being affiliated with WKYT in Lexington, WYMT carried lots of news originated by the Lexington station. Barbara Clark of WKYT suddenly appeared on the television talking about the ACFesV and did an interview with Harlan Mayor Fred Knapp. After this was over the station continued with other Kentucky news, but nothing at all about an explosion in Harlan County.

General Jung looked solemnly at General Rhee. Jung said, "We both know if your mission was successful it would be all over the news. It failed!"

"That's not possible," General Rhee replied. "That farm is pretty remote. Very likely no one heard or saw the explosion. I'm sure it'll be reported later."

"Better be," said Jung. He then looked at Pretty Boy and said, "Mr. Maggard, it's been a very long night. We'd greatly appreciate your taking us to the motel and we'll get a little rest before we start our journey back home."

"Be happy to," Pretty Boy replied. "But I was told to change your license tags from Indiana to Georgia." He reached over and grabbed the Georgia plates. "It'll just take a few seconds. After I do that we'll be on our way to the motel."

The generals nodded. The four walked out to their vehicles.

• • •

Same Day, noon
New Hope Baptist Church
Harlan, Kentucky

Pastor Raymond Bell had just finished his sermon at the morning worship service. Attendance was excellent, hardly an empty seat. As the congregation exited the church Raymond shook hands and thanked his flock for attending. Several stood together at the foot of the steps waiting for the pastor, including Raymond's wife Betty, Dr. Randy Peters, Mayor Fred Knapp, Deputy Kyle Potter, his mother Carolyn, and Sheriff Sterling.

The weather was perfect. It was sunny and about 70 degrees. White, fluffy clouds filled the sky, and there was a light breeze blowing. It was chamber of commerce weather.

After the last worshipers had been greeted, Pastor Bell walked down the steps and joined the group. He said to them, "I want to thank each of you for attending this morning." He then looked with a smile at Bert and Randy and added, "I know some of you had a very active evening last night and busy morning today."

Bert spoke up, "That's true, pastor." He went on to detail for everyone what had taken place last night at the Slusher farm and this morning at the Memorial.

Fred said, "Wow, wow, and wow! I'd say you have been busy indeed. Do you know how Trigger and Fatso are doing?"

"Yeah, I stopped by the hospital after I got cleaned up for church. They were both still very weak but were doing well. Their doctor told me they should be fine in a couple of days. He treated their head wounds and said they were dehydrated and about starved, and had lots of cuts and bruises mainly from the bindings on their hands and feet. But our prayers were answered."

He continued, "One thing I wanted to ask of each of you. Please keep quiet about the fake anchor crosses. We don't want that news to get out. We said the Memorial was closed today because of a safety issue. Randy will be heading there in just a few minutes. He will go in the Memorial alone carrying his briefcase. He will ask the state troopers from the helicopter to wait outside while he gathers the anchor crosses. He'll lollygag in the Memorial for a few minutes and then come out carrying his empty briefcase, lock the door, and be escorted back to the helicopter and then on back home to Lexington. No one will ever know that the fake artifacts were stolen. That's the way we want to keep it."

Kyle asked, "What about the hole in the floor and the tunnel?"

Bert replied, "I'm going to work a deal with Bob and Bud Rehsa to close off the tunnel and fill the hole in the Memorial and pour new concrete atop it. I'm sure the brothers will agree to keep everything confidential."

The rest of the group nodded approval.

Betty Bell asked, "You think you'll ever catch the 10 Koreans?"

"I doubt it, Betty," said Bert. "But when Kim Jong-un finds the anchor crosses are fake he'll likely give those soldiers some well deserved punishment."

"No bad turn goes unpunished," the mayor said.

Pastor Bell looked at him and said, "I think that's a new one, Fred."

Fred smiled and said, "No, but I did hear one before church this morning that seems appropriate to tell right now. This Lutheran pastor always started off each worship service with the phrase, *'The Lord be with you'*. The congregation would then always respond, *'and also with you'*. One Sunday the sound system didn't seem to be working right. The pastor stepped up to the pulpit and said, *'There's something wrong with this microphone'*. The people said, *'and also with you'*."

The group erupted in laughter. Pastor Bell said, "Got to remember that one. Thanks mayor."

Fred said, "Glad you liked it. I've got to get back over to the festival. It winds up this afternoon. And I just know it's going to finish perfectly....in spite of those North Korean guys."

All gave hugs and shook hands, and then went their separate ways.

• • •

Same Day, 3:15 pm
Harlan County Court House
Harlan, Kentucky

The festival had just concluded. Mayor Fred Knapp had delivered the final speech in which he appologized to everyone for having to close the Seibert Memorial Building today because of safety issues. He assured everyone that all the anchor crosses were just fine and would be back on display at next year's festival. After his conclusion message the crowd started to disperse. The mayor walked off the stage and down the Court House steps to several of his friends who were chatting.

With a big smile Fred walked up and said, "A great success. A great success. Everyone agree?"

Kyle and Carolyn Potter, Betty and Raymond Bell, and Sheriff Sterling all nodded in agreement. "It was another stunning success, Mr. Mayor," Betty Bell said. "Harlan is certainly blessed to have you organize it every year. It seems to continue to grow."

Kyle Potter said, "True. And even with those nutcase Koreans trying to disrupt it. I don't think a single attendee realized anything those Koreans were doing. It was a wonderful festival."

Bert said, "I agree. And thanks not only to Fred, but also to all the planning committee members. Now that ACFesV is all put to bed I promised Carolyn that she and I would take a nice Sunday afternoon drive up to Black Mountain to see the fall leaves. They should be at their peak in color right now and I know it will be a beautiful drive."

Carolyn walked over, took Bert's hand, and said, "I've been very much looking forward to this drive." She looked up into his eyes and said, "I'm all ready. Let's hit the road."

All waved bye to them as they started walking toward the sheriff's car. Bert said, "And when we get to the top of Black Mountain I have an important question I want to ask you."

Carolyn looked surprised. She thought a moment and replied, "Well, I'm sure I'll have an important answer to that question!"

● ● ●

Monday, October 5, 8:30 am
Sheriff's Office
Harlan, Kentucky

Rosie looked up when she heard the entrance door open. She saw Bert walking in and said, "Good morning, you're running a tad late today."

Bert reached up and gave Preacher Puss a nice pet and said, "Yeah, I was a bit behind on my sleep. I did manage to get caught up a little. But here I am, reporting for work."

Rosie replied, "No problem. Preacher Puss and I have everything under control. No action from any bad guys this morning."

"That's good to hear," the sheriff said as he continued walking through the reception area toward his office.

Preacher Puss suddenly jumped down from her shelf and started running toward Bert. She passed him and went to the door going into his office. She sat down with her back against the door and started to meow loudly.

Rosie said, "I don't have a clue what that cat is up to now."

Bert reached down and gave her several nice strokes. He then reached for the door. Preacher Puss jumped straight up and grabbed the sheriff's hand as he was turning the knob. Bert released it and grabbed the cat with his other hand, holding her in his arms.

He looked inquisitively at her and said, "Preacher Puss, I do believe I'm getting the message that you don't want me to open that door."

"That's exactly what I think too, Bert," shouted Rosie. "And you know that cat has instincts beyond belief. I sure wouldn't open the door."

Preacher Puss started to meow loudly again and looked straight at Bert.

"I agree," he said. He turned and gently placed the cat on the floor. "I'm going around and come in my office through the back door. Maybe there's something in there that Preacher Puss wants me to see."

"Great idea," Rosie replied. "You be extra careful. Those Koreans could still be around here."

Bert tapped the gun in his holster and said, "Will do." He walked out the door going to the back.

After unlocking the back door he entered and started walking toward his office. The moment he entered it he saw the bomb taped to the floor beside the closed door going into the reception area. He quickly walked over to it and clicked the door lock so that no one could open it. He then walked to his desk, sat down, punched the intercom and said, "Rosie, don't be alarmed, but there's a bomb in here attached to my door. I've locked it, so it can't be opened, and looking at the bomb I noticed there is a trip wire attached to it and the door. So I'm pretty sure the bomb will explode only if someone tries to open the door. Call the state police and tell them to send the bomb squad here. In the meantime, grab Preacher Puss and go outside. I'll meet you there and we'll wait on the state police.

"Right. We're out of here," Rosie replied. She jumped up, ran to the door, reached up and grabbed the cat, and went out and stood in the Court House lawn.

In a couple of minutes Bert joined her. He looked at Preacher Puss and said, "Can you believe it? That cat has done it again! She's unquestionably saved our lives this morning Rosie."

After another 5 minutes they heard the siren, and then the state police bomb wagon pulled up. Two troopers jumped out and came over. Bert said, "Follow me." He led them around and through the back door to his office. They examined the bomb and then requested that he go back outside while they disenabled it. He walked back out to Rosie.

A few minutes later the two troopers came out carrying the bomb. They placed it in a large, bomb-proof box in their vehicle, and then walked over to Bert, Rosie, and Preacher Puss. Trooper #1 said, "Sheriff, it was a big one. Had you or anyone opened that door just an inch or so it would have triggered a massive explosion. Could well have been big enough to even kill other folks in the Court House building."

Trooper #2 smiled and said, "You must have gone to church yesterday!"

Bert smiled and said, "I sure did." He then told the two troopers how Preacher Puss had prevented him from opening the door this morning.

All four looked at the cat, gently swishing her tail while curled in Rosie's arms. Both troopers gave her a nice pet. She purred approvingly.

Trooper #1 said, "We've heard all the stories about Preacher Puss. What an amazing animal." She meowed loudly as they turned and left..

•••

Same Day, 9 pm
Brunswick Landing Marina
Brunswick, Georgia

The two Korean vehicles had just arrived at the marina. All 10 men had gotten out and were standing in the parking lot.

General Jung said, "The good news is we made it to Brunswick. The bad news is that we listened to the car radio the entire trip and heard absolutely no news report on any explosions in Harlan County." He looked solemnly at Rhee and Yi and said, "If either of those bombs had worked as planned the news would be on all the stations.

Nothing at all about an explosion at the Slusher farm, and nothing at all about Sheriff Sterling being blown up. You have failed!"

Rhee and Yi looked down and remained quiet.

Jung then looked at the brief case in his hand and said, "At least my team accomplished their mission. We do have the golden anchor crosses. So all is not lost."

Captain Juan came running up to them and said, "Good, good, good. You are here. The Island Time awaits you. Please, grab your luggage and let's get moving."

Everyone walked out on the dock and boarded the boat. The mate cast off the lines. They were on their way to Havana.

Chapter 17

Tuesday, October 6, 9 am

Creech Cafe

Harlan, Kentucky

Bert, Kyle, and Fred were sipping coffee at their back table. Fred looked at the sheriff and said, "Bert, the good Lord was certainly looking over you yesterday morning. And not just you, but Rosie and Preacher Puss as well."

Bert replied, "Was He ever! And His messenger was Preacher Puss!"

Kyle and Fred laughed and nodded agreement.

"Those North Koreans are nothing but ruthless killers," Kyle said.

"Want-to-be killers," replied Bert with a smile. "Fortunately for us they only succeeded in stealing some fake anchor crosses....and they don't even know that!"

Fred nodded and said, "So I guess ole Kim Jong-un's not as smart as we are!"

"I'm sure he'll be raving mad when he discovers the fakes. I wouldn't want to be near him when that happens," said Kyle.

Bert said, "Well, looking back we sure do have lots for which to be thankful. The festival was a huge success and all the attempts by the North Koreans were failures. That's as good as it gets."

Bennie walked up with the coffee pot and refilled everyone's cup. He said, "I heard a good one this past weekend. Anyone care to hear it?"

Bert replied, "Sure Bennie. We're all ears."

He said, "There was this guy named Will J. Cooney who just loved to play tricks on people. One day he was walking down the street and ran into a guy he knew who wasn't very bright. He stopped him, handed him a card with letters and numbers on it. He told the guy, whose name was Alonzo, that the writing on the card was a very special code that would make any person reading it into a devoted friend immediately. Alonzo took the card, thanked Will, and went on his way. A couple of days later Will ran into

Alonzo again and saw that he was covered with bandages. He asked what happened. Alonzo frowned at Will and said he just gave the card to his worst enemy. He read it and then really got mad and worked me over. Will laughed and told Alonzo it was just a joke."

Kyle said, "Okay, okay. So what did the card say?"

Bennie handed him the card:

370H55V

0773H

All three looked at it. Each shook their head. Kyle said, "I still don't get it."

Bennie replied, "Turn it upside down!"

Kyle was holding the card. He turned it upside down, all three read it, and the men started cackling. Kyle said, "I guess Alonzo handed the card upside down!"

Bert said, "Bennie, you are getting better, but you need to keep practicing. You've still got a ways to go to catch up with Fred."

Bennie took the card back and said, "Fred, is it okay if I tape this card to the wall?"

"Only if you don't tape it upside down," replied Fred with a smile.

Bennie nodded and walked away.

Fred then turned to Bert and said, "I remember last Sunday after church you told Carolyn you were going to take her for a drive up Black Mountain to see the leaves. How did it go?"

Bert smiled and said, "Perfect. The leaves were brilliant. We caught them at their absolute peak. And that wasn't even the best part of the trip."

Fred and Kyle looked expectantly. Bert put his finger up across his lips and said, "Can't tell you right now. You both plan on being in church this Sunday?

Both nodded positively.

"Then on Sunday, as Paul Harvey used to say, you'll learn the rest of the story!"

Kyle scratched his head and said, "That's strange. I asked mother the same question after the trip and she giggled and she said the same thing."

Fred looked at Kyle and said, "Guess we'll just have to wait till Sunday."

Bert smiled triumphantly. He then said, "The two G-men stopped by the office yesterday afternoon to say their good-byes. They were on their way back to D.C. I told them what had just happened there in my office that morning, and they were really surprised. Both guys said they couldn't wait to tell all the stories when they got back to D.C. They added that Preacher Puss would be elevated to super celebrity status. Said to tell you both good-bye, and they spent several minutes petting and talking with Preacher Puss on their way out."

"They're good guys," the mayor said. "What about Joe Chang? Is he going to head to D.C. also?"

"No," Bert replied. "The G-Men said that Mr. Lee had offered Joe Chang half ownership in The China Pan. As I understand it, Joe told Mr. Lee he would have to decline the offer because he just didn't have the funds. Apparently Mr. Lee liked Joe so well that he made him an offer he just couldn't refuse, he financed it for him. Joe told the G-Men that he really liked Mr. Lee, the work there, and all the friendly people in Harlan. He accepted the offer and will be staying on. You now have another taxpaying citizen here in Harlan, Mr. Mayor."

Fred smiled and gave a thumbs-up.

He then asked, "Do you have an update on Trigger and Fatso?"

Bert replied, "Yeah. I called the hospital before I left the house this morning. The doc said they were discharged late yesterday. He said they recovered very quickly, and that they planned to return to work today. I think I'll drive to their grocery this afternoon and check on them."

"Give them my regards," Fred said.

"And mine too," said Kyle.

"I certainly shall," Bert replied. "One last question, Fred, before Kyle and I get to work. Do you think you can top Bennie's story this morning?"

Fred looked over to where Bennie was standing behind the cash register, and leaned in close to the two lawmen. He whispered, "Here's a good one I just heard. This lady just loved to sing. She decided she would try out for the church choir, but thought first she'd better practice every evening for the next week. So each evening after dinner she would start to sing at the top of her lungs. The family dog would always chime in and howl loudly. After several nights of this the lady's husband shouted and asked her if she would please sing songs the dog didn't know."

"Another good one, Mr. Mayor," Bert said, as he and Kyle stood and departed Creech's headed to work."

● ● ●

Same Day, 2 pm
Maggard's Grocery
Near Wallins, Kentucky

Trigger Green was chatting with Fatso at the checkout counter. The front door opened and in walked Sheriff Sterling.

"Hey Bert, good to see you," Trigger shouted.

Bert walked over to them and said, "You two look mighty good. A big change from the last time I saw you."

Everyone shook hands.

Fatso said, "We feel a lot better too. It seems like all I've done for the past two days has been to drink water and eat. I don't know how much longer we could have made it. You saved our lives, Bert."

Trigger nodded and said, "And that's exactly how I feel too. Thanks so much, my friend."

"Well, it did work out well," the sheriff replied. "I just wanted to drop by to make sure you guys were okay."

"Appreciate your concern," Trigger said. "Fatso and I feel real bad that we actually helped those guys get all situated. But we honestly didn't know they were planning all those terrible things. There's no way I would agree to help someone hurt or kill people. But that's all water over the dam now. I take it they're all gone and we'll likely never see them again."

"I guess," Bert replied. "We have no idea where they are. But I have a strong feeling they are not in Harlan county!"

He continued, "I did want to ask a favor. We're wanting to keep the tunnel business under wraps. I can honestly assure you that the Koreans did not get the anchor crosses. Dr. Peters has all six of them at his Center in Lexington. For several reasons, we just don't want the public to know about their digging the tunnel to the Memorial. I'm arranging with the Rehsa brothers to fill it in. When they get finished no one will be able to tell it was ever there. And they will agree to hold it in confidence as well. Is that okay with you two?"

"No problem at all," Trigger said. "We'll certainly keep quiet about it."

"Great," Bert said. "Well, just wanted to check on you. I better head back to Harlan. You guys have a good day." He turned and started toward the door.

Fatso yelled, "Hey Bert, you know how to make an elephant fly?"

Bert kept walking.

"You start with a 3 foot zipper," Fatso said with a chuckle.

Bert laughed and walked out to his cruiser.

●●●

Same Day, 10 pm
City Marina
Havana, Cuba

Captain Juan carefully maneuvered Island Time into her slip. After his mate had secured the docking lines he shouted to everyone down in the cabin, "Hit the deck. We've landed in Havana. Let's get the van loaded and get you guys to the airport."

The three generals came up first, followed by the 7 soldiers. Each was carrying his luggage. They all walked off the boat onto the dock.

General Yi then pulled on General Jung's sleeve and said, "Hold up just a minute, General Jung. General Rhee and I would like to discuss something with you."

Jung, looking agitated and surprised, said, "What is it. We need to get to the airport."

Yi said, "You and your men do. General Rhee, Choe, and Park have discussed our situation and have decided to stay in Havana. We know that because our missions failed we will be executed if we return to Pyongyang. Kim Jong-un does not tolerate failure. We four have no families, so he cannot take his revenge on them. During the trip from

Brunswick we have talked with Captain Juan, and told him our plans to remain here. He has agreed to help us find employment and will allow us to sleep on Island Time until we get settled. You and your men have had a successful mission, and I know the Supreme Leader will reward you handsomely. We are truly sorry that our missions failed. We don't understand why, but apparently they did. We wish you and your men the very best, and hope you understand."

Jung looked very surprised. He thought for a minute and said, "I do understand. And I think your decision is wise. If you don't mind, I think it would be best if I told Kim that you four overpowered us here in Havana and vanished. Otherwise, he might think we helped you escape. Is that okay?"

Rhee said, "Sure. Tell him anything you wish. Havana's a big place. Anyone he might send will not find us."

All the Koreans then slapped each other on the back, shook hands, and separated. Jung, his five men, and Captain Juan headed to the airport where the Koreans would board Kim's jet to Pyongyang. Yi, Rhee, Choe, and Park went back aboard the Island Time for a good night's rest.

• • •

Thursday, October 8, 6 pm
The China Pan
Harlan, Kentucky

Carolyn and Bert were seated in a booth in one corner of the restaurant. No one else was seated nearby.

Bert said, "Honey, Fred may get jealous if he finds out we're eating here so much."

"I think he'll understand," she said with a smile. "We've just been here a few times, and always for dinner. I think he might get jealous if we were frequently having lunch here."

Joe Chang walked up and said, "You're being here again tonight must mean you like my cooking."

Bert said, "Indeed. Your food is superb. And I understand from the grapevine that you and Mr. Lee are now co-owners. Congratulations!"

Joe replied, "I am greatly honored. Mr. Lee is a very good man. It has worked out *well* for me. I love my job and this restaurant, and I love all the people I've met in Harlan. They seem to accept me. I am truly blessed. And you're responsible for getting me this job, Bert. Otherwise i'd likely be back in Washington right now without a job or friends. I'm a very lucky man. Thank you so much."

"You deserve it, my friend. I'm so pleased it worked out for you," Bert said.

Joe shook hands with both Bert and Carolyn, and started to go back to the kitchen. Bert said, "By the way, I wanted to extend a personal invitation to you to visit at New Hope Baptist Church this Sunday. I understand there's going to be a very important announcement made there."

Joe looked a bit surprised and said, "Sheriff, I certainly could not turn down an invitation from you. I will see you Sunday. Thanks."

Joe returned to the kitchen. Bert looked at Carolyn, patted her hand, and winked.

Chapter 18

Saturday, October 10, 10 am
Pyongyang, North Korea

Kim Jong-un sat in his throne chair overlooking the parade ground in front of his palace. The table beside him was full of food wrappers. He had just polished off five egg McMuffins. He had an enormous smile on his face. Hundreds of thousands of North Koreans were assembled before him. The military parade had started at 8 am and had continued until now. All his latest military equipment, including rockets and launchers, had passed by. His military jet fighter planes had flown overhead. Thousands of soldiers had marched goose-stepping in front of him.

But now came the highlight. General Jung and his five soldiers marched out on the parade ground directly in front of their Supreme Leader. Each was dressed in their finest uniforms, adorned with metals that rivaled those worn by Ethiopia's Haile Selassie. All strutted until they were exactly in front of their Supreme Leader. They then turned toward him and smartly saluted. Kim, with great difficulty, stood and saluted back.

The six soldiers turned and formed a straight line, standing side by side. Each then reached into his pocket and pulled out a beautiful golden anchor cross. They each held the anchor cross at their side in their right hand. Kim's special ceremony band started to play.

Kim looked at the grandstand down below that had been constructed to allow world press representatives a ring-side seat at the ceremony. When his announcement had gone out hundreds of newspeople accepted his invitation and were in attendance. Almost every country was represented. Some had also sent political leaders. These mixed in with the press. Kim had proclaimed in the announcement that at this ceremony he would unveil the key that would allow him to achieve world dominion. That moment had arrived.

Six more decorated soldiers marched out and lined up facing General Jung and his five men. They stood only about 30 feet apart. Each carried a high powered rifle. One soldier carrying a rifle stood facing one soldier carrying an anchor cross.

The band played louder. The enormous crowd grew silent. Kim Jong-un beamed from his palatial perch.

On cue, General Jung and each of his men raised their right hand and positioned the anchor cross over their heart. Simultaneously, the soldiers with the rifles raised them into firing position, each aimed directly at the center of an anchor cross.

The music stopped. The silence was deafening.

Suddenly there were six loud blasts from the rifles. Six bullets pierced an anchor cross and then through the soldier holding it. General Jung and his men slumped to the ground.

A great murmur went through the crowd. Kim's jaw dropped, his face began to turn beet red. He suddenly began jumping up and down and shouting at the top of his lungs, "No, no, no, this cannot be. Those artifacts are suppose to protect those possessing them."

Other than Kim's raving, the only sound that could be heard were the clicking of the cameras from the world press photographing the dead soldiers. The videos they had taken would be too graphic to show.

Kim turned, pushed over his throne and table, and walked in disgust back into his palace. He and his country had been humiliated. It was almost more than he could endure. He secluded himself in his bedroom and ordered lunch, four Big Mac's, three large fries, and two chocolate milk shakes.

●●●

Same Day, 9 am

Creech Cafe

Harlan, Kentucky

Fred, Bert, and Kyle had just taken seats at their table after watching a special report on the television in Fred's office. The report showed what looked like a firing squad in the front of Kim's palace. It showed six soldiers lined up holding golden anchor crosses across their hearts, and then smoke emerging from the rifle barrels. The video stopped, and the next image was a photograph showing the six dead soldiers. You could also see several of the anchor crosses with holes in them. The last video recorded Kim Jong-un having a temper tantrum and them storming back into his palace.

All three men were laughing loudly. Bert said, "That's the best television I ever saw. Ole Kim Jong-un sure was upset!"

"Yeah," A smiling Kyle replied. "I guess his plans for world dominion just went down the drain."

Fred looked at his watch. He said, "9 in the morning here right now. That means that it's 6 in the evening in Pyongyang. I guess all that happened just a few hours ago. I bet ole Kim is still steaming. I wonder how many he will execute?"

Bert replied, "Well, he started with Jung and his five comrades....although it wasn't anticipated to be an execution. No telling how many more will die. He was seriously embarrassed."

Kyle said, "I'm sure not feeling sorry for him. He got what he deserved, and so did Jung and his men. I'm just glad it's over, and we know the outcome!"

Fred and Bert nodded.

Bennie rushed up with the coffee pot and cups. After placing one in front of each man and filling them he said, "You guys sure seem happy this morning. Fred must have told you a good one."

Bert and Kyle looked toward Fred. Bert said, "No, but I'll bet a month's wages that he's getting ready to."

Bennie waited to hear the story along with Bert and Kyle.

Fred grinned and started, "Heard this one yesterday. This lady brings her pet rabbit, Fluffy, in to see the vet.

The vet places the rabbit on the examination table and after looking at it he tells the lady Fluffy is dead. The lady goes nuts. She jumps up and down and tells the vet that he didn't even do anything and that he's a terrible pet doctor. The vet rolls his eyes and then walks out of the room. In a minute he comes back with a golden Labrador retriever. The dog puts his front paws on the table and sniffs around the rabbit from head to toe. He then looks up at the vet with very sad eyes and shakes his head. The vet pets the dog and then takes him out of the room. In a minute he's back bringing a large gray cat. The cat jumps up on the examination table and delicately sniffs all around Fluffy, shakes his head, meows loudly, and strolls out of the room. The vet then tells the lady that he's really sorry that Fluffy is dead. He then turns to his computer, hits a few keys, and produces a bill for the lady. She looks at it and screams. She says she's not paying $500, and tells the vet he did nothing for Fluffy. The vet tells the lady if she had taken his word when he told her the rabbit was dead the bill would have only been $25. But with the Lab report and Cat scan it's now $500!"

Bennie roared with laughter and said, "Fred, I'll never catch up with you. That was a good one." He walked away with the coffee pot.

Fred looked at Bert and Kyle and said, "Guys, I think we've now got a wrap on ACFesV, and thankfully the bad guys once again lost out. We have so much to be thankful for."

Kyle and Bert nodded. Bert said, "You're sure right there, Fred. We all need to go to church tomorrow and praise the Lord for our many blessings." He then winked at Kyle and Fred as he stood to walk across the street.

• • •

Sunday, October 11, noon
New Hope Baptist Church
Harlan, Kentucky

Pastor Bell had just concluded the morning worship service. The church was packed, not a vacant seat. Several people were standing in the back.

After the closing prayer the pastor looked out at the congregation with a shy smile and said, "I'd like to think this overflowing attendance today is attributable to my sermon." He paused for a moment and continued, "But I think the word got out that my good friend Sheriff J. Bert Sterling had an announcement to make, and he chose to make it at the conclusion of today's service."

Pastor Bell then looked at Bert and Carolyn sitting on the front row holding hands. Bert first stood and then walked to the pulpit. Raymond Bell took his seat.

Bert looked out at the congregation, cleared his throat, smiled sheepishly, and said, "Friends, I do in fact have an announcement. But I'd better get off on the right foot, so Carolyn would you kindly come up and join me."

Carolyn stood with a big smile, nodded, and then walked up to the pulpit to join Bert. When she got there they held hands.

Bert continued, "As some of you know, last Sunday Carolyn and I took a drive to Black Mountain to enjoy the fall foliage. Once we reached the top I pulled the car over, parked, and we got out to look around. As most of you also know, Carolyn and I have been good, I should say very good, friends for many years now. For the past several years we have dated, and I have grown to love her very much. I told her this and, remarkably, she said she felt a similar love for me. I then asked if she would be my wife."

Applause broke out in the church. The congregation started cheering and all stood up.

Carolyn and Bert embraced and kissed with tears streaming down their faces.

www.ingramcontent.com/pod-product-compliance
Lightning Source LLC
Chambersburg PA
CBHW021135110726
47900CB00002B/357